The Arcane Academy - The Shattered Veil

The Arcane Academy, Volume 4

Kirsten Yates

Published by Kirsten Yates, 2024.

This is a work of fiction. Similarities to real people, places, or events are entirely coincidental.

THE ARCANE ACADEMY - THE SHATTERED VEIL

First edition. November 27, 2024.

Copyright © 2024 Kirsten Yates.

ISBN: 979-8230959489

Written by Kirsten Yates.

Table of Contents

Chapter 1: Whispers of the Rift 1
Chapter 2: A Fractured Sky 4
Chapter 3: The Relic of Shadows 8
Chapter 4: An Unexpected Alliance 12
Chapter 5: The Forbidden Passage 16
Chapter 6: The Shimmering Gate 21
Chapter 7: The Battle at the Crystal Spire 26
Chapter 8: The Obsidian Forest 30
Chapter 9: The Shadow King 34
Chapter 10: The Relic's Echo 38
Chapter 11: Trials of the Veil 42
Chapter 12: The Forgotten Ritual 46
Chapter 13: Secrets of the Academy 50
Chapter 14: The Betrayal 54
Chapter 15: The Gathering Storm 57
Chapter 16: The Heart of the Veil 61
Chapter 17: The Shattered Alliance 65
Chapter 18: A World in Peril 69
Chapter 19: The Final Ritual 73
Chapter 20: The Veil Restored 78
Chapter 21: A New Dawn 82
Chapter 22: The Legacy of the Veil 86
Chapter 23: The Nexus Unveiled 90
Chapter 24: The Trials of Unity 94
Chapter 25: The Trial of Flames 98
Chapter 26: The Crystal Cavern 103
Chapter 27: The Awakening of the Ancients 107
Chapter 28: The Temple of the First Magic 111
Chapter 29: The Ancients' Awakening 115
Chapter 30: The Last Stand 118

Chapter 1: Whispers of the Rift

It was a quiet morning at the Arcane Academy, but something in the air felt different. Ivy stood by the tall, arched window of the North Tower, watching the rolling mist over the academy grounds. The usual hum of magic that coursed through the air seemed off—distant, as though retreating into some unreachable space. Her instincts told her that something was wrong.

The warmth of the morning sun should have been comforting, but it barely pierced the strange haze clinging to the sky. Ivy could sense the tension, the unease that crept through the walls of the Academy like a forgotten whisper. Students moved through the hallways with furrowed brows, glancing nervously at the sky. It was as though the very heart of magic had faltered.

"Ivy, do you feel it too?" Aiden's voice startled her. He had appeared by her side, his eyes scanning the horizon.

She nodded. "It's like the magic is... different. It's faint, like it's slipping away."

Aiden's brow furrowed. "I overheard Professor Veldren talking with Headmistress Evelynn. Something about the Veil weakening."

Ivy's pulse quickened at the mention of the Veil. The Veil was the barrier between their world and the Shadow Realm, a mysterious and dangerous parallel realm. For centuries, it had kept their world safe, preventing the dark magic from bleeding into the Arcane Academy and beyond.

"Do you think it's just a rumor?" Ivy asked, her voice barely a whisper.

"That's what I thought until I saw this," Aiden said, pulling a small shard of glowing crystal from his cloak. The crystal pulsed faintly with a violet light, but it flickered irregularly, as if it were struggling to maintain its glow.

"Where did you get that?" Ivy asked, her eyes wide.

"It was found near the Western Gate, right where the boundary of the Veil begins. It's like the magic there is... fraying." He hesitated before adding, "The professors won't say it, but I think the Veil is starting to break."

Ivy felt a chill run down her spine. If the Veil was weakening, it could mean the merging of their world with the Shadow Realm, a catastrophe no one was prepared for.

At that moment, the deep chime of the Academy's bell echoed through the halls, signaling an emergency gathering. Ivy and Aiden exchanged a glance before hurrying down the winding staircase to the Great Hall.

The hall was filled with students, their hushed conversations buzzing with confusion. Headmistress Evelynn stood at the front, her sharp eyes scanning the crowd. Her usual calm expression was replaced with a look of grave concern. Behind her, the professors stood in a tight line, their faces tense.

"Students of the Arcane Academy," the Headmistress began, her voice amplified by a subtle spell. "We are facing a matter of great urgency. As some of you may have noticed, there have been disturbances in the flow of magic throughout the Academy. After thorough investigation, it has been confirmed that the Veil protecting our world from the Shadow Realm has begun to weaken."

Gasps rippled through the hall. Ivy felt a knot tighten in her chest. It was true. The Veil—their last line of defense—was failing.

THE ARCANE ACADEMY - THE SHATTERED VEIL

Headmistress Evelynn raised her hand to silence the crowd. "We do not know the full extent of the damage yet, but steps are being taken to investigate the cause. In the meantime, all students are to remain within the Academy grounds until further notice. The magical wards around the Academy will hold, but we must be vigilant. I urge you all to continue your studies with diligence. Prepare yourselves for whatever lies ahead."

Ivy's mind raced. The Veil breaking was the worst possible outcome. The Shadow Realm was a place of chaotic magic, inhabited by beings that thrived on destruction. If the Veil fell, everything they knew would be at risk.

As the students began to disperse, Ivy turned to Aiden, her voice low. "We need to figure out what's causing this. We can't just sit and wait for the Veil to break completely."

Aiden nodded. "Agreed. I have a feeling this goes deeper than anyone realizes."

As they left the Great Hall, Ivy's mind was already racing with questions. What was behind the weakening of the Veil? And more importantly, how could they stop it before it was too late?

The whispers of the Rift had begun, and Ivy knew that their world was on the brink of something far more dangerous than they could imagine.

Chapter 2: A Fractured Sky

The tension in the Arcane Academy had only grown since Headmistress Evelynn's announcement. Classes continued as usual, but an underlying current of anxiety rippled through the halls. Ivy could feel it in the air—an unsettling hum, as though magic itself was out of sync.

Days after the emergency gathering, Ivy and Aiden stood on the sprawling lawns just outside the Academy, gazing at the sky. The sun had begun to set, casting an eerie, orange glow across the horizon. But it was not the sunset that caught their attention.

A thin, jagged crack had appeared in the sky.

"Is that—?" Aiden started; his voice barely audible.

"It wasn't there this morning," Ivy finished, her eyes wide. The crack shimmered with faint light, almost like a tear in fabric. It was as though the sky itself was breaking apart.

"Something's coming through," Aiden whispered, his voice tense with urgency. "The Veil's really collapsing."

Ivy nodded, her heart pounding. If the crack was connected to the Veil, it meant that the barrier between their world and the Shadow Realm was starting to fracture. How long before the two realms collided completely?

Suddenly, a cold breeze whipped through the courtyard, swirling leaves, and dust around them. The hairs on the back of Ivy's neck stood up as a faint pulse of dark energy radiated from the crack, sending a chill down her spine.

"Come on, we need to tell Headmistress Evelynn," Aiden urged, already turning back toward the Academy.

But just as they were about to move, a flash of light burst from the crack, illuminating the entire sky with a blinding brilliance. Ivy shielded her eyes, her heart hammering in her chest. A low rumble echoed across the courtyard, vibrating the ground beneath their feet.

Then, as quickly as it had appeared, the light faded, leaving behind only silence.

"What was that?" Ivy asked breathlessly, lowering her hand from her eyes.

Aiden looked equally shaken. "I don't know, but it felt like—"

A loud *crack* interrupted him, and both turned to see a figure stumbling out of the forest just beyond the Academy grounds. The figure, cloaked in tattered black robes, collapsed onto the grass, breathing heavily.

"Is that... a student?" Ivy asked, her eyes narrowing as she tried to get a closer look.

"No," Aiden replied, his voice grim. "Look at his robes. He's not from the Academy."

The two hurried over to the fallen figure, who lay motionless, his face hidden beneath the shadow of his hood. Ivy knelt beside him, cautiously pulling back the hood to reveal a young man, his face pale and gaunt, as if drained of life. His eyes fluttered open, filled with fear and exhaustion.

"The Rift," he rasped, his voice barely audible. "It's... broken."

Ivy leaned closer, her pulse quickening. "Who are you? Where did you come from?"

The man's eyes widened in panic. "The Shadow Realm," he whispered. "The Veil is shattering. They are coming..."

Before Ivy could ask anything more, his eyes rolled back, and his body went limp. Ivy checked his pulse—he was alive, but barely.

"We need to get him to the Headmistress," Aiden said, already helping Ivy lift the unconscious stranger.

Together, they hurried back toward the Academy, their minds racing with questions. Who was this man, and how had he crossed into their world? Was the crack in the sky the beginning of something far worse?

As they reached the main entrance, the heavy doors swung open, and Headmistress Evelynn stood there, her face as calm and composed as ever. But her eyes—those sharp, all-knowing eyes—betrayed a flicker of concern.

"What is this?" she asked, her gaze shifting from Ivy and Aiden to the unconscious stranger in their arms.

"He came through the forest," Ivy said quickly. "He said... he said the Rift is broken, and that they're coming."

For a moment, the Headmistress remained silent, her eyes narrowing slightly as she studied the man. Then, with a wave of her hand, she summoned two professors to take the stranger away.

"Bring him to the infirmary," she instructed them. "Make sure he is treated with the utmost care. I will need to speak with him once he regains consciousness."

Once the professors disappeared with the stranger, the Headmistress turned back to Ivy and Aiden, her expression unreadable.

"It seems our situation is more dire than I feared," she said quietly. "The crack in the Veil has begun to widen."

Ivy felt a knot tighten in her chest. "What does that mean for us? For the Academy?"

"It means we are running out of time," Headmistress Evelynn replied, her voice laced with tension. "The crack you saw in the sky is just the beginning. If the Veil shatters completely, the Shadow Realm will bleed into ours, and we will be defenseless against its forces."

Aiden clenched his fists. "How do we stop it?"

The Headmistress regarded them for a long moment before speaking again. "There may be a way to repair the Veil, but it will require great sacrifice. The answers lie deep within the Arcane Archives, in ancient texts long forgotten. I will need your help to uncover them."

Ivy and Aiden exchanged a glance, their resolve hardening.

"We'll do whatever it takes," Ivy said firmly.

Headmistress Evelynn nodded. "Then prepare yourselves. The answers we seek may be dangerous to uncover, but they are our only hope."

As they made their way to the Archives, Ivy glanced back at the crack in the sky. It was still there, shimmering faintly in the darkening twilight. The air felt heavy with magic, as though something ancient and powerful was stirring beneath the surface.

The fractured sky was a warning, and Ivy knew that whatever lay beyond the Rift was growing closer with every passing moment.

Chapter 3: The Relic of Shadows

The Arcane Archives were buried deep beneath the Academy, a labyrinth of forgotten knowledge and ancient magic. The air grew colder as Ivy and Aiden descended the stone steps, the torches on the walls flickering with an eerie blue flame. The weight of history pressed in on them, the silence only broken by the distant echo of their footsteps.

"Are you sure we'll find what we need here?" Aiden asked, glancing at the endless rows of ancient tomes and scrolls.

Ivy nodded, though she was not entirely certain. "If there's anything that can help us repair the Veil, it'll be hidden in these texts. We just have to find the right one."

The Headmistress had given them little guidance, only mentioning that they needed to locate a specific text that referenced an artifact known as the *Relic of Shadows*. According to legend, this relic held the power to control and mend the forces of the Shadow Realm. If it was real, it could be their only hope of restoring the Veil before it shattered entirely.

But the Archives were vast and full of forgotten secrets. Finding one obscure text could take days—if not weeks.

As they reached the central chamber, Ivy spotted a stone pedestal in the middle of the room. Upon it rested an ancient, tattered scroll, its edges frayed with time. Strange symbols were carved into the pedestal itself, glowing faintly with dark energy.

THE ARCANE ACADEMY - THE SHATTERED VEIL

"This must be it," she whispered, stepping closer to the pedestal.

Aiden frowned. "It feels... off. Do you sense that?"

Ivy did. The closer she got to the scroll, the more she could feel a strange pull—like the air around it was thicker, heavier. A chill ran down her spine as she reached out toward the ancient parchment.

Just as her fingers brushed the surface, the torches in the room flickered and dimmed, casting long shadows across the stone walls. A low hum vibrated through the chamber, followed by a whispering voice, ancient and sinister.

"Beware... the Relic of Shadows..."

Ivy recoiled, her heart pounding. She exchanged a nervous glance with Aiden, who looked just as unsettled.

"You heard that, right?" she asked, her voice barely above a whisper.

"Yeah," Aiden replied, his eyes scanning the dark corners of the room. "We need to be careful. This place is... alive."

Swallowing her fear, Ivy carefully lifted the scroll from the pedestal. The moment she did, the glowing symbols on the stone faded, and the eerie hum subsided. The whispers, however, remained, like the faint echoes of long-dead spirits.

Unfurling the scroll, Ivy studied the faded text. It was written in an ancient language, one she recognized from their studies but could barely read.

"It mentions the Relic," she said slowly, tracing her finger along the delicate script. "It says the Relic of Shadows was created to bind the power of the Rift, to keep the balance between the worlds."

Aiden leaned over her shoulder, squinting at the text. "And there, it says the Relic was lost during the Great Sundering. No one knows where it is now."

Ivy frowned. "But there has to be a clue, some way to find it."

As she scanned the rest of the scroll, her eyes landed on a symbol at the bottom—a jagged line running through a circle, surrounded by runes. It was the same symbol she had seen in her dreams, just before the Veil had begun to weaken.

"I've seen this symbol before," Ivy said, her voice low. "In my dreams, right before the Veil started to fracture."

Aiden raised an eyebrow. "You think it's connected?"

"I don't know, but I'm starting to think the Veil isn't the only thing at risk here." Ivy's mind raced. "What if the Relic isn't just about mending the Veil? What if it is the key to something even bigger?"

Before Aiden could respond, a loud crash echoed through the chamber, followed by the distinct sound of heavy footsteps.

"Someone's coming," Ivy whispered urgently, rolling up the scroll and tucking it into her satchel.

They quickly ducked behind one of the towering bookshelves just as the doors to the Archives slammed open. Ivy peeked through the narrow gap between the shelves, her heart pounding as she saw three figures enter the room, all clad in dark robes.

At the front of the group was Professor Selene, the Academy's enigmatic Mistress of Shadows. Her pale face was framed by jet-black hair, and her eyes glowed faintly with a dangerous, dark magic. Behind her were two other professors, their faces hidden beneath their hoods.

"I can sense the disturbance," Professor Selene said, her voice cold and commanding. "The students are close to discovering the truth."

One of the hooded figures spoke. "Do you think they've found the Relic?"

Professor Selene's lips curled into a thin smile. "If they have, it will only hasten their demise. The power of the Relic is not something they can control."

Ivy's blood ran cold. *Professor Selene knows about the Relic?*

"Should we stop them?" the second hooded figure asked.

"No," Selene replied with a dismissive wave of her hand. "Let them think they're one step ahead. By the time they realize the true nature of the Relic, it will be too late."

With that, the three professors turned and left, their footsteps fading into the distance. Ivy and Aiden remained hidden, both too stunned to move.

"She knows," Aiden whispered. "Selene knows about the Relic. And if she is involved..."

"Then we're not just dealing with the Veil breaking," Ivy finished, her voice trembling. "We're dealing with something much worse."

The stakes had just risen. They were not only racing against the clock to stop the Veil from shattering—they were up against an enemy within the Academy itself.

As Ivy and Aiden slipped out of the Archives and back into the darkened halls, Ivy clutched the scroll tightly in her hands. The Relic of Shadows held the key to saving—or dooming—their world. But now, it was clear they were not the only ones searching for it.

And the shadows were closing in fast.

Chapter 4: An Unexpected Alliance

The tension in the air was palpable as Ivy and Aiden hurried back to the main halls of the Arcane Academy. Their minds raced with the revelation about Professor Selene—one of the most trusted professors in the school—and her sinister knowledge of the Relic of Shadows. The more they thought about it, the more dangerous it seemed. They were in over their heads, and the clock was ticking.

"We need help," Aiden muttered, his voice filled with urgency. "We can't take on Selene alone. If she is after the Relic, who knows what she will do?"

Ivy nodded; her brow furrowed in concentration. "But who can we trust? If Selene is part of this, there could be others."

They had to be careful. Trust was fragile now, and one wrong move could put everything at risk. But they could not do this alone, and Ivy knew it.

As they entered the courtyard, the dim moonlight casting long shadows across the stone pathways, a figure stepped out from behind one of the archways. Ivy's hand instinctively went to her wand, ready for anything.

"Wait," Aiden said, his eyes widening. "It's Rowan."

Rowan Nightshade, one of the Academy's top students, stood before them, his silver-gray eyes gleaming in the faint light. Known for his sharp intellect and mastery over illusion magic, Rowan was a student no one ever quite trusted. His powers were potent, but his motives were often unclear.

"Ivy, Aiden," Rowan greeted them with a calm smile, though there was an edge of seriousness in his voice. "You've been busy."

Ivy narrowed her eyes. "How do you know what we've been up to?"

Rowan stepped forward, lowering his voice. "I know a lot more than you think. And I know you're looking for the Relic of Shadows."

Aiden tensed. "If you're working with Selene—"

"I'm not," Rowan interrupted, his expression hardening. "I don't trust Selene any more than you do. But I am not here to fight you. I want to help."

"Why?" Ivy asked, suspicious. Rowan was not exactly the type to help of the goodness of his heart. There had to be something in it for him.

"Because," Rowan said, his voice growing quieter, "if Selene gets her hands on the Relic, none of us are safe. She is not just looking for power—she is looking to control the entire Academy. Maybe even more than that."

Ivy exchanged a wary glance with Aiden. Rowan's words rang true, but trusting him was a risk. He was known for playing both sides of a situation, manipulating the outcome to his advantage. Still, Ivy could not shake the feeling that they might need him.

"You know where the Relic is, don't you?" Ivy asked, testing him.

Rowan's eyes flickered with something—a hint of amusement, perhaps. "I don't know where it is exactly, but I have a lead. There is a hidden chamber beneath the school. It has been sealed off for centuries, but I've... found a way in."

Aiden crossed his arms. "Why not go after the Relic yourself, then?"

"Because," Rowan replied smoothly, "the magic protecting the chamber isn't something I can break alone. It requires more than just illusion magic. It requires something ancient, something connected to the original founders of the Academy."

Ivy's heart skipped a beat. "The founders' magic..."

"Exactly," Rowan confirmed. "Which is why I need you two. You have access to parts of the school that I do not. Together, we might be able to find the chamber and the Relic before Selene does."

Aiden glanced at Ivy. "What do you think?"

Ivy considered their options. They were short on time, and without Rowan's knowledge of the hidden chamber, they would be stumbling in the dark. As much as she did not fully trust him, they could not afford to turn him away.

"Alright," Ivy said, her voice firm. "We'll work together. But if you betray us—"

"I won't," Rowan said, cutting her off with a rare look of sincerity. "We're all in this together now."

With their unlikely alliance forged, Rowan led them deeper into the Academy's underground tunnels, away from the main halls and into the oldest parts of the school. The air grew colder, the stone walls damp with moisture and thick with the scent of ancient magic.

"The chamber is somewhere beneath here," Rowan explained, stopping in front of an ornate stone door. It was covered in intricate runes, glowing faintly with an otherworldly light. "The door's sealed by powerful wards. It will take all of us to break through."

Ivy studied the runes, recognizing some of the symbols from her studies. These were no ordinary wards. They were designed to repel intruders with deadly force.

"Stand back," Rowan said, pulling out a vial of shimmering liquid from his cloak. "This will weaken the wards just enough for us to break through."

He poured the liquid onto the stone, and the runes sizzled, flickering as the wards began to falter. Ivy and Aiden raised their wands, focusing their magic on the weakened door.

"Together," Ivy said, her voice steady.

THE ARCANE ACADEMY - THE SHATTERED VEIL

With a surge of energy, their combined magic struck the door, shattering the last of the wards. The stone creaked and groaned, slowly swinging open to reveal a dark passageway beyond.

As they stepped into the chamber, a strange energy filled the air. The walls were lined with ancient murals, depicting battles between mages and shadowy figures. At the far end of the room, resting on a stone altar, was a small, black orb—the Relic of Shadows.

Ivy's heart pounded as she approached the Relic. It was smaller than she had imagined, but the dark energy radiating from it was palpable, almost alive.

Before she could reach for it, Rowan grabbed her arm. "Careful," he warned. "The Relic is dangerous. If we take it, Selene will know."

"What do we do?" Aiden asked, his eyes darting between the Relic and the exit.

Rowan's gaze darkened. "We take it, but we do it on our terms. With this Relic, we'll have the power to stop Selene... or destroy everything if it falls into the wrong hands."

As Ivy stood before the Relic of Shadows, the weight of their mission pressed down on her. The line between friend and foe was thinner than ever, and the choices they made in the coming days could determine the fate of the entire Academy.

One thing was certain: their unexpected alliance had brought them closer to the truth, but the real danger was still ahead.

Chapter 5: The Forbidden Passage

The air in the underground chamber hung heavy with the scent of ancient dust and old magic. Ivy, Aiden, and Rowan stood before the black orb—the *Relic of Shadows*—as its dark energy pulsated like a living heart. Despite Rowan's warnings, Ivy could not take her eyes off it. It called to her, pulling her closer with an invisible force.

"We can't just leave it here," Ivy said, her voice barely above a whisper. "Selene will find it."

Rowan stepped forward; his expression serious. "I know, but taking it is not as simple as you think. There are traps—curses woven into the magic of this place. One wrong move and we are done for."

Aiden nodded. "Then we need to figure out how to disarm the traps before Selene makes her move."

Rowan's sharp gaze swept the room. His knowledge of the Academy's hidden corners had already proven invaluable, but even he seemed wary of what lay ahead. "There is one place we need to go before we can safely remove the Relic. It is dangerous, and it is forbidden to students—"

"Of course it is," Aiden cut in, raising an eyebrow. "Is anything at this school *not* forbidden?"

Rowan smirked. "Fair point. But the *Forbidden Passage* is different. It is hidden deep beneath the Academy, older than the school itself. It was sealed centuries ago after something... dark... was discovered inside. Something that can undo the wards protecting the Relic."

THE ARCANE ACADEMY - THE SHATTERED VEIL

Ivy felt a chill run down her spine. The *Forbidden Passage*—it was a name spoken only in whispers among the students, a place no one dared to speak of openly. She had heard of it during her first year, a tale meant to frighten students into staying on the safer paths. But she had always assumed it was just a legend.

"Why would the Passage have anything to do with the Relic?" Ivy asked, skepticism edging her voice.

"Because it's where the original founders of the Academy sealed away the most dangerous magic they encountered," Rowan explained. "The Relic was not the only thing tied to the Shadow Realm. The Passage holds the key to unlocking the full power of the Relic... or destroying it."

Aiden looked uneasy. "And how exactly are we supposed to get into a place no one's been in for centuries?"

Rowan held up a key. It was small, carved from a dark, crystalline substance that shimmered in the dim light of the chamber. "I've already taken care of that."

Ivy exchanged a glance with Aiden, her pulse quickening. They had no other choice if they wanted to stop Selene.

"Alright," she said, determination settling in her chest. "Lead the way."

The journey to the *Forbidden Passage* was fraught with silence and unease. Rowan led them through a series of hidden staircases and narrow tunnels that twisted beneath the Academy's foundations. The deeper they went, the colder the air became, and the stone walls seemed to pulse with a faint, magical glow, as if the very structure of the school was alive and watching them.

After what felt like hours of descending, they arrived at a large iron door, ancient and covered in thick vines of dark magic. The door was etched with strange symbols that seemed to shift and writhe under their gaze.

"This is it," Rowan said, stepping forward. "The *Forbidden Passage*."

Ivy's heart pounded in her chest as she stared at the door. There was something deeply unsettling about the aura it radiated, as though it held a malevolent presence waiting to be unleashed.

Rowan carefully inserted the crystal key into a small, almost invisible keyhole. As the key turned, the ancient door groaned, and the symbols lit up with a fiery orange glow. With a loud creak, the door slowly swung open, revealing a long, dark corridor.

The air inside the Passage was colder than anything Ivy had ever felt. It was as though they had stepped into a void, where time itself stood still. The walls were lined with stone statues—grim figures of mages and warriors, all frozen in expressions of horror.

Aiden swallowed hard. "Those statues... They look like—"

"People," Rowan finished grimly. "Those who tried to pass through here and failed."

Ivy felt a wave of nausea rise in her throat but forced herself to stay focused. "What exactly are we looking for?"

Rowan led them down the corridor, his voice barely audible over the eerie silence. "There is a chamber at the heart of the Passage. Inside, there is a glyph—an ancient rune of power. We need to activate it to dispel the curses surrounding the Relic. But be warned... once we are inside, the Passage will test us."

"Test us how?" Aiden asked, his tone sharp with suspicion.

Rowan's face darkened. "The Passage reveals your greatest fears. It tries to break you."

Ivy's heart raced. She had faced fear before, but something about this place felt far more sinister. She tightened her grip on her wand, steeling herself for what lay ahead. "Let's get this over with."

They pressed on, the darkness growing thicker with every step. The oppressive atmosphere made it difficult to breathe, and the statues lining the walls seemed to whisper in the distance, their stone faces twisted in agony. Ivy could feel the Passage working on her already, creeping into her mind, stirring up old fears and doubts.

At last, they reached the central chamber. It was a vast, circular room with a high ceiling, illuminated only by the faint glow of the ancient glyph etched into the floor. The walls were covered in intricate carvings, depicting scenes of battles between light and shadow, order, and chaos.

"This is it," Rowan said, stepping toward the glyph. "We must activate it together. But once we do, the Passage will react. Stay focused, no matter what you see."

Ivy nodded, taking a deep breath. She knelt beside Rowan, her fingers hovering above the glowing glyph. Aiden followed suit, and together, they began to channel their magic into the ancient symbol.

For a moment, nothing happened.

Then, the ground beneath them trembled.

A low, rumbling sound echoed through the chamber, and the shadows on the walls began to move, coiling and shifting like living creatures. Ivy's heart raced as a cold dread washed over her.

Suddenly, the shadows surged forward, engulfing the room in darkness.

Ivy's vision blurred, and the sound of her own heartbeat filled her ears. She heard distant voices—familiar, yet distorted. Faces from her past appeared in the shadows, twisted with fear and malice. Old memories, old mistakes, came rushing back to her, each one sharper and more painful than the last.

Aiden's voice broke through the haze. "It is an illusion! Focus on the glyph!"

Ivy clenched her fists, forcing herself to block out the haunting images. She channeled more magic into the glyph, the energy burning through her veins. The shadows recoiled, but they did not retreat. Instead, they grew more aggressive, swirling around her like a storm.

"Ivy!" Aiden shouted; his voice strained with effort. "We have to finish this now!"

With one final push, Ivy poured everything she had into the glyph. The light from the symbol exploded outward, flooding the chamber with blinding brightness. The shadows screamed, writhing, and dissipating into the ether.

Then, as quickly as it had begun, the nightmare ended.

The chamber was still and silent once more. The glyph on the floor now pulsed with a steady, calming light.

"It's done," Rowan said, his voice hoarse. "The curses surrounding the Relic should be broken."

Ivy collapsed to her knees, exhausted but relieved. They had passed the test, but the toll it had taken on them was clear.

"We're one step closer," Ivy whispered, wiping the sweat from her brow. "But the real battle is just beginning."

As they made their way back to the surface, Ivy could not shake the feeling that the Passage had revealed more than just her fears. It had shown her something deeper, something she could not yet understand.

The path ahead was darker than ever, but there was no turning back now.

Chapter 6: The Shimmering Gate

The wind howled through the night as Ivy, Aiden, and Rowan approached the clearing at the edge of the Forbidden Forest. The towering trees seemed to bow under the weight of the magic in the air, their gnarled branches reaching like skeletal hands toward the stars. At the heart of the clearing stood the *Shimmering Gate*, an ancient portal long forgotten by most of the Arcane Academy.

The moonlight reflected off the gate's surface, casting eerie, dancing patterns of light across the ground. The structure was made of a metal so ancient it had lost its luster, now glowing faintly with residual magic. It was shaped like an archway, standing at least ten feet high, and though it appeared solid, the space within the arch shimmered like water in the wind.

"This is it," Rowan said, his voice low with awe. "The *Shimmering Gate*. A portal between worlds."

Ivy stared at the gate, her pulse quickening. She had read about it in the forbidden section of the library—an ancient relic used by the first mages to travel between realms. But it was said to be unstable, unpredictable, and impossible to control.

Aiden glanced at Rowan, frowning. "You're sure this will get us to the Relic's origin?"

Rowan nodded, though there was a trace of uncertainty in his eyes. "The Shimmering Gate leads to the *Ethereal Realm*. It is where the founders of the Academy first encountered the magic that created the

Relic of Shadows. If we can find the source of that magic, we can stop Selene from fully unlocking its power."

Ivy stepped closer to the gate, her heart thudding in her chest. She could feel the energy emanating from it, a mixture of danger and excitement. She had always craved adventure, the thrill of the unknown, but this... this was something else. The Ethereal Realm was a place no living mage had visited in centuries. It was a realm of pure magic, where the boundaries between reality and illusion blurred.

"I don't suppose there's any guarantee we'll make it back?" Ivy asked, her voice a mix of nerves and anticipation.

Rowan shook his head. "No guarantees. But if we do not go, Selene will beat us there. She already knows about the Gate."

Aiden stepped up beside Ivy, his expression resolute. "Then we're going."

Rowan retrieved a small vial from his cloak, filled with a swirling blue liquid. "Before we enter, you need to drink this. It is a stabilizing potion. The Ethereal Realm has... effects on mortals. The potion should protect us from being overwhelmed by the raw magic there."

One by one, they drank the potion. It tasted bitter, leaving a strange tingling sensation on their tongues. Ivy immediately felt her senses sharpen, the world around her becoming clearer, more vibrant. The magic in the air no longer felt oppressive but instead hummed in tune with her own energy.

Rowan approached the gate and raised his hand toward it. With a flick of his wrist, the shimmering surface rippled like water disturbed by a stone. The portal sprang to life, the surface shifting and changing, revealing glimpses of a world beyond. Swirling clouds of mist, shimmering light, and distant mountains made of pure crystal.

"Stay close," Rowan instructed, stepping toward the portal. "Once we cross, the Ethereal Realm will start testing us. It is not a place that follows the rules of our world. It adapts to our fears, our desires."

THE ARCANE ACADEMY - THE SHATTERED VEIL

Without hesitation, Rowan stepped through the gate. Aiden followed, casting one last glance at Ivy, who took a deep breath and steeled herself.

The moment Ivy stepped through the gate; the world shifted around her. It was as though she had been plunged into a pool of liquid light. Her vision blurred, and for a moment, she felt weightless, her body floating through a sea of color and sound. She could hear whispers, faint and indistinct, like a distant song carried on the wind.

Then, with a sudden jolt, her feet touched solid ground.

Ivy blinked, her senses reeling as the world came into focus. They were no longer in the Forbidden Forest. Instead, they stood on a vast, endless plain of shimmering silver grass, stretching as far as the eye could see. Above them, the sky was a swirling vortex of colors—purple, gold, and blue—moving in slow, hypnotic patterns. Strange creatures, half-formed and translucent, floated in the distance, their shapes constantly shifting and changing.

The air here was thick with magic, so dense that Ivy could feel it buzzing against her skin, making her every breath feel electric.

"This... is the Ethereal Realm," Aiden breathed, wide-eyed as he took in the surreal landscape.

Rowan was already scanning the horizon, his expression tight with concentration. "We need to find the *Crystal Spire*. It is the heart of this realm, and it is where the founders first bound the magic that created the Relic. If we are going to find a way to stop Selene, that is where we will do it."

As they began to move through the shimmering grass, Ivy could not shake the feeling that they were being watched. The creatures in the distance never seemed to come closer, yet she could feel their eyes on her. The air itself seemed to shift with every step they took, as though the realm was responding to their presence.

After what felt like hours of walking, the landscape began to change. The silver grass gave way to a forest of towering crystal trees, their branches glowing faintly in the strange, multicolored light. The ground beneath their feet shifted from soft earth to smooth, polished stone.

And there, in the distance, rising above the trees like a beacon, was the *Crystal Spire*.

It was enormous, a towering structure of pure crystal that shimmered in every color of the spectrum. Its surface was covered in intricate runes, pulsating with energy. Ivy could feel the power radiating from it, even from this distance.

"That's it," Rowan said, his voice tense. "The source of the Relic's magic."

But as they approached the base of the Spire, something changed. The air grew colder, and the light from the Spire dimmed. Ivy felt a chill run down her spine as a shadow passed over the ground in front of her.

From the trees, a figure emerged.

It was cloaked in black, its face hidden beneath a hood, but Ivy could feel the malevolent energy radiating from it. The figure raised its hand, and the shadows around them seemed to come alive, swirling and coiling like serpents.

"Who dares trespass in the Realm of the Shadows?" the figure's voice echoed, cold and hollow.

Ivy's heart pounded in her chest. They had come too far to turn back now.

"We're here to stop you," Rowan said, stepping forward, his hand gripping his wand tightly. "You can't have the Relic's power."

The figure's laugh was low and cruel. "You are fools to think you can defy the will of the Shadows. The Relic's power belongs to us, and soon, it will be mine."

Ivy tightened her grip on her wand, preparing for the fight she knew was coming.

The Shimmering Gate had brought them to the heart of magic itself, but it seemed that their journey had only just begun.

THE ARCANE ACADEMY - THE SHATTERED VEIL

And the battle for the Relic was far from over.

Chapter 7: The Battle at the Crystal Spire

The dark figure stood unmoving, but the air around it seemed to ripple with unseen power. Ivy felt her pulse race, her hand trembling slightly as she tightened her grip on her wand. Beside her, Aiden and Rowan stood ready, their eyes locked on the shadowy figure that now blocked their path to the Crystal Spire.

"Stay together," Rowan muttered under his breath. "We don't know what we're up against."

The figure in black raised its hand, and with a flick of its wrist, the shadows that had been swirling around the base of the trees rushed toward them. Ivy felt the air grow cold as the dark tendrils snaked across the ground, twisting, and curling like living things. Instinctively, she raised her wand.

"Deflecto!" she shouted; her voice strong despite the fear gnawing at her insides.

A shimmering shield of light erupted from her wand, surrounding her and her companions. The shadowy tendrils struck the barrier with a hiss, recoiling as if burned. But the figure in black did not relent. With another wave of its hand, the shadows intensified, pressing harder against Ivy's shield.

"Ivy, it's not enough!" Aiden shouted, his own wand glowing as he summoned a blast of energy toward the figure. The spell hit the figure's cloak, but it dissipated as if it had struck nothing but smoke.

"We have to get to the Spire!" Rowan called out, his eyes darting between the figure and the towering crystal structure behind them. "It's the only way we can sever the connection to the Relic!"

Ivy gritted her teeth, pushing more of her energy into the shield. She could feel the strain as the shadows continued to batter against it, and beads of sweat formed on her brow. The Ethereal Realm pulsed with magic, but here, in the presence of the dark figure, it felt twisted, corrupted.

A sudden blast from Aiden's wand pushed the shadows back momentarily, giving them a brief opening.

"Now!" Rowan yelled, making a break for the Spire. Ivy and Aiden followed close behind, their feet pounding against the polished stone floor as they sprinted toward the base of the Crystal Spire. The figure moved to follow, its form gliding effortlessly across the ground, but it seemed to hesitate for a moment as they neared the Spire.

Ivy glanced back and saw it stop just short of the shimmering light that radiated from the crystal structure. The figure raised its hand, but instead of attacking, it pointed directly at them. Ivy felt a surge of dark energy wash over her, and a voice echoed in her mind.

You cannot hide from the shadows. They will find you.

She stumbled slightly but shook off the sensation as they reached the base of the Spire. The towering crystal was even more imposing up close, its surface covered in glowing runes that seemed to pulse in time with the beating of her heart. Rowan did not hesitate. He raised his wand and began muttering an incantation, his voice steady and deliberate.

Ivy and Aiden positioned themselves on either side of him, their eyes scanning the area for any sign of the dark figure. But the figure remained at a distance, watching them with an eerie stillness.

As Rowan's spell grew in intensity, the runes on the Spire began to glow brighter. The ground beneath them trembled, and a low hum filled the air. Ivy could feel the raw power of the Ethereal Realm surging through the Spire, its energy building to a crescendo.

Suddenly, a deep crack echoed through the clearing. Ivy's heart skipped a beat as she saw a fissure form along the surface of the Spire, spreading rapidly upward. The light from the crystal intensified, flooding the clearing with a brilliant, blinding glow.

"Ivy, help me!" Rowan shouted; his voice strained. "The Spire's resisting! It is protecting the Relic's power!"

Without thinking, Ivy raised her wand and joined in the incantation. She could feel the magic flowing through her, merging with Rowan's as they worked to contain the energy surging from the Spire. The fissure in the crystal deepened, and Ivy realized with a jolt of fear that the Spire was on the verge of collapsing.

"Hold on!" Aiden called out; his voice barely audible over the roar of the magic swirling around them.

But then, just as Ivy felt the last of her strength beginning to wane, the light from the Spire shifted. It became softer, more controlled, as if responding to their efforts. The fissure stopped spreading, and the ground beneath them steadied.

Rowan let out a sigh of relief, his hand lowering as the incantation came to an end. "We did it. The connection's been severed."

For a moment, everything was still. The Spire stood intact, its glow returning to a calm, steady pulse. But Ivy knew it was not over. She could still feel the presence of the dark figure behind them, watching.

As they turned to face it, the figure remained motionless, its hooded face hidden in shadow. But Ivy sensed a shift in its demeanor. The oppressive weight of its magic had lessened, though it still radiated danger.

"You may have severed the Spire," the figure said, its voice low and menacing. "But the Relic's power still flows. You are too late to stop what has already begun."

Ivy narrowed her eyes. "We'll find a way to stop you. We're not done yet."

The figure let out a low, chilling laugh. "You misunderstand, child. I am not your enemy. I am merely a messenger."

Before any of them could react, the figure began to dissolve into shadow, its form unraveling like smoke in the wind. As it faded, its final words echoed through the clearing.

"The true darkness has yet to reveal itself."

Ivy felt a chill crawl down her spine as the figure disappeared completely. Silence settled over the clearing, broken only by the faint hum of the Crystal Spire.

"What did it mean?" Aiden asked, his brow furrowed in confusion.

Rowan shook his head, his expression grim. "I don't know. But whatever it is, we need to find out before it's too late."

Ivy looked back at the Spire, the weight of the figure's words lingering in her mind. The battle was not over. Far from it. The Relic was still out there, and with it, the shadow that threatened not just the Academy, but the entire magical world.

And the darkness that awaited them was far more dangerous than anything they had faced before.

Chapter 8: The Obsidian Forest

The wind howled through the jagged black trees as Ivy, Aiden, and Rowan stepped cautiously into the Obsidian Forest. The sharp, darkened branches reached up to the sky like twisted claws, casting eerie shadows on the ground. The forest had an unnatural stillness, broken only by the occasional rustling of unseen creatures scurrying through the dense underbrush.

"This place gives me the creeps," Aiden muttered, glancing around warily. His hand never left his wand, ready for any threat that might emerge from the darkness.

"It's not just the forest," Ivy said, her voice low. "Something's watching us."

Rowan nodded in agreement, his eyes scanning their surroundings. "The Obsidian Forest is cursed. Legend says it was once a place of light and magic, but something dark took root here, corrupting everything. The Academy's archives speak of ancient guardians who once protected the forest's heart—but that was before the Rift."

The air felt heavier as they ventured deeper, and Ivy could feel the oppressive magic thickening around them. It was not just any magic—it was ancient, darker than anything she had encountered before. Each step felt like a trespass into a forbidden realm, where every movement, every sound, was being tracked by unseen forces.

THE ARCANE ACADEMY - THE SHATTERED VEIL

Rowan pulled out a crumpled piece of parchment, the ancient map that had guided them this far. "We need to find the Heart of the Forest. That's where the path to the Obsidian Gate will be."

Aiden raised an eyebrow. "The Obsidian Gate? Sounds like a welcoming place."

"Hardly," Rowan replied, his tone serious. "The gate is said to lead to another realm, a pocket of magic beyond our understanding. It's where the Relic of Shadows was hidden, sealed away centuries ago."

Ivy shivered at the thought. They had been searching for the Relic for weeks, but every lead had only taken them deeper into danger. Now, with the dark figure's cryptic warnings still echoing in her mind, the stakes felt higher than ever.

Suddenly, the ground beneath them shook, a deep rumble that seemed to come from the very heart of the forest. Ivy stumbled, barely catching herself against a nearby tree.

"What was that?" Aiden asked, his voice tense.

Rowan looked up; his expression grim. "The Forest is waking up."

Before Ivy could ask what, he meant, the trees began to move. The branches twisted and writhed, their shadows shifting like serpents. The dark bark cracked and splintered, revealing veins of glowing crimson energy that pulsed through the trees like blood.

"We're not alone," Ivy whispered, her eyes darting around as the shapes of creatures began to emerge from the shadows. They were not like any animals she had ever seen before—these were beings of darkness, their eyes glowing red, their forms twisted and monstrous.

The creatures let out low, guttural growls as they closed in on the trio, their movements unnaturally fluid and silent. Ivy felt her heart race as she raised her wand, her mind racing to remember a spell powerful enough to fend them off.

"Back-to-back!" Rowan ordered, his own wand already glowing with energy. "We can't let them surround us."

The creatures charged all at once, a mass of shadow and claws. Ivy reacted instinctively, unleashing a blast of light that pushed the nearest creature back. It screeched in pain as the light seared its dark form, but more took its place, lunging at them with deadly speed.

"Ventus Obscura!" Aiden shouted, sending a whirlwind of dark wind toward the creatures. The force of the spell knocked several of them back, but they quickly regrouped, their red eyes glowing with malevolent intent.

Rowan's wand flicked with precision, casting barrier after barrier, but the creatures were relentless. One of them leapt toward Ivy, its claws outstretched. She barely managed to deflect it with a burst of magic, but the impact sent her stumbling.

"They're too many!" Ivy gasped, panic rising in her chest. "We have to get out of here!"

Rowan's eyes narrowed as he cast another spell, creating a dome of light that momentarily halted the creatures' advance. "There's no running. We have to reach the Heart, or they'll keep coming."

"Then we need a plan!" Aiden said, his voice strained as he cast another spell to fend off an advancing creature. "Because this isn't working!"

Ivy's mind raced. The creatures were drawn to their magic, but there had to be a way to use that against them. Her eyes flicked to the glowing veins in the trees—the source of the forest's corruption.

"The trees!" she shouted. "They're connected to the creatures somehow! If we can sever the link, we might stop them!"

Rowan glanced at her, realization dawning in his eyes. "The magic flowing through the forest—it's feeding the creatures."

Without hesitation, Rowan aimed his wand at the nearest tree, its bark glowing with dark energy. "Olivero's!"

A wave of magic shot from his wand, striking the tree and severing one of the glowing veins. The crimson light flickered and dimmed, and Ivy noticed the nearest creatures faltering, their movements slowing.

"It's working!" Ivy said, casting her own spell toward another tree. The pulse of energy cut through the forest, and more of the creatures began to retreat, their forms dissolving back into shadow.

Aiden followed suit, and soon the forest was filled with the sound of cracking wood and dissipating shadows. The creatures, once aggressive and unstoppable, now slinked back into the darkness, their connection to the corrupted magic broken.

For a moment, all was silent.

The trio stood panting, their wands still raised, scanning the forest for any sign of the creatures. But the danger seemed to have passed—for now.

"Let's not do that again," Aiden muttered, lowering his wand.

Rowan nodded, his face pale but determined. "We're close to the Heart. It's just beyond that ridge."

As they moved deeper into the Obsidian Forest, Ivy could not shake the feeling that something even darker awaited them. The forest's corruption was only part of the mystery, and whatever lay at the Heart of the Forest would either be their salvation—or their doom.

But one thing was clear: the Relic was within reach, and with it, the final key to unlocking the true power of the Rift.

Chapter 9: The Shadow King

The temperature dropped noticeably as Ivy, Aiden, and Rowan approached the Heart of the Obsidian Forest. The trees thinned out, revealing a large clearing, and at its center stood a monolithic structure—an obsidian throne, black as night, with veins of crimson energy pulsing through its surface. Sitting on the throne was a figure draped in shadow, his eyes glowing a deep, malevolent red.

Rowan halted, his breath catching in his throat. "The Shadow King."

The presence of the being sitting on the throne was suffocating, a darkness that weighed down on them like a heavy cloak. The air itself seemed to bend around him, thick with the taint of ancient magic. Ivy could feel it pressing against her chest, making it hard to breathe.

"Stay close," she whispered, gripping her wand tightly. "This is what the forest has been hiding."

The Shadow King shifted, his form twisting like living smoke. His voice was a low, chilling rasp, echoing in the stillness. "So, the children of light dare to step into my domain."

Ivy felt a shiver run down her spine. The creature's gaze locked onto her, and for a moment, it felt as though he was staring into the depths of her soul. Every instinct screamed at her to run, but she stood her ground, refusing to give in to the fear tightening in her chest.

"We're here for the Relic of Shadows," Rowan said, his voice steadier than Ivy expected. "We know it's hidden here, and we won't leave without it."

The Shadow King chuckled darkly. "The Relic of Shadows? You seek power you do not understand, child. That which you desire is more than a mere artifact. It is a fragment of the Abyss itself."

Aiden took a step forward, his jaw clenched. "We don't care about your riddles. Hand it over."

The Shadow King's eyes flared with amusement. "You have spirit, boy, but you are gravely mistaken. You think you can challenge me? The Heart of this Forest, the shadows that lurk within, all bow to me. I am their king, and soon, I will be more."

Rowan raised his wand, his voice filled with determination. "We'll see about that."

Before anyone could react, Rowan unleashed a spell—an arc of pure light aimed directly at the Shadow King. But before it could reach its target, the darkness surrounding the throne surged forward, swallowing the spell as if it were nothing more than a flicker of flame.

Ivy's heart sank. The Shadow King had not even flinched.

"You have made a mistake," the Shadow King hissed, his voice carrying a new edge of malice. "You are in my realm now. My power is absolute."

With a wave of his hand, the shadows around the throne came to life. Tendrils of darkness snaked toward them, faster than they could react. Ivy barely had time to raise her wand before one of the tendrils wrapped around her ankle, pulling her toward the ground. She struggled, her wand glowing with a desperate blast of magic, but the darkness only tightened its grip.

Rowan and Aiden were faring no better. The shadows wrapped around them, dragging them toward the center of the clearing where the Shadow King watched with a cruel smile.

Ivy felt panic rising in her throat as the cold tendrils reached her chest, constricting her breath. She knew she had to do something—anything—before the darkness consumed them entirely. Her mind raced, searching for a spell, a plan, a way out.

Then she remembered what they had learned in the Academy's archives.

"The Heart," she gasped, struggling to speak. "The Heart of the Forest... it's... it's his anchor. If we break it—"

Rowan's eyes widened in realization. "It's how he controls the shadows!"

But the Shadow King heard them. His eyes narrowed, and with a flick of his wrist, the shadows constricted even further, silencing them.

"Do you think I am so easily defeated?" he whispered, rising from his throne. "I have ruled these lands for centuries. I have seen the rise and fall of kings, wizards, and heroes. None have challenged me and lived to tell the tale."

He raised his hand, and Ivy felt the tendrils around her tighten to the point of agony. Her vision blurred, and darkness threatened to close in. But through the haze of pain, she could still see the Heart of the Forest, pulsing with the same crimson light that glowed in the Shadow King's eyes.

With the last of her strength, Ivy reached out with her magic. She focused on the pulsating energy, pushing through the overwhelming darkness that surrounded them. She felt her magic connect with the Heart, the ancient power surging through her.

"No!" the Shadow King roared, sensing what she was doing.

But it was too late.

Ivy's magic clashed with the energy of the Heart, and for a moment, everything was still. Then, with a deafening crack, the ground beneath the throne split open, and a blinding light burst forth. The Heart of the Forest shattered, its magic exploding outward in a wave of force that sent the Shadow King stumbling back.

THE ARCANE ACADEMY - THE SHATTERED VEIL

The tendrils of shadow dissolved, releasing Ivy, Aiden, and Rowan from their grip. The clearing was filled with the sound of cracking trees and rushing wind as the Obsidian Forest began to collapse in on itself. The throne crumbled, and the Shadow King, his form flickering like a dying flame, let out a roar of fury.

"You may have broken the Heart," he growled, his voice echoing with rage. "But the Relic will still be mine. The shadows are eternal."

With that, his form dissolved into a swirl of darkness, vanishing into the void. The oppressive weight of his presence lifted, but Ivy knew he was not gone for good. He would return, more dangerous than ever.

The clearing fell silent, the only sound the distant hum of magic fading from the shattered Heart of the Forest.

Aiden staggered to his feet, breathing heavily. "Well... that was fun."

Rowan nodded, though his expression was grim. "We've delayed him, but the Relic is still out there. We need to find it before he does."

Ivy wiped the sweat from her brow, her heart still pounding in her chest. "He'll be back, and next time, we might not be so lucky."

They had won this battle, but the war against the Shadow King had only just begun. And now, they knew just how high the stakes were.

As they turned to leave the Obsidian Forest, Ivy glanced back at the shattered Heart. The darkness that had once ruled this place was broken, but the threat of the Shadow King still loomed over them, a shadow that would follow them until the Relic was found—or destroyed.

Chapter 10: The Relic's Echo

The journey out of the Obsidian Forest was silent, save for the soft crunch of leaves underfoot. The once vibrant magical energies that pulsed through the trees were now muted, the forest left in eerie stillness after the Heart's destruction. Ivy could still feel a lingering darkness in the air, a faint echo of the Shadow King's presence, as though he was watching them from afar.

Rowan led the way, his brow furrowed in deep thought. Aiden followed close behind, glancing over his shoulder every few minutes, as if expecting the shadows to come alive again. Ivy walked in the middle, her mind spinning with everything that had happened. They had shattered the Heart, but the Shadow King's warning echoed in her mind.

"The Relic will still be mine. The shadows are eternal."

"We need to move faster," Rowan said suddenly, breaking the silence. "The Shadow King may have retreated for now, but he'll return once he regains his strength."

Aiden let out a frustrated sigh. "And where do we even begin? We still don't know where the Relic of Shadows is."

Ivy pulled the ancient map from her cloak, the same one that had led them into the heart of the Obsidian Forest. The parchment was old, its edges frayed, but the magical runes that marked their path were still glowing faintly.

"This map led us here," Ivy said, tracing the lines with her finger. "It must show us the next step."

Rowan glanced at the map, nodding thoughtfully. "The Relic's power is immense. It was hidden away to keep it from falling into the wrong hands. But we are not dealing with just any dark magic. The Shadow King is tied to the Abyss itself. Wherever the Relic is, it's bound to him—and he'll do anything to get it back."

Aiden crossed his arms, his brow furrowed. "So, we're walking into another trap? Great."

"We don't have a choice," Ivy said, meeting his gaze. "If the Shadow King gets his hands on the Relic, he'll unleash a power that could destroy not just the Academy, but the entire world. We have to stop him."

Aiden sighed, running a hand through his hair. "Yeah, I know. I just wish we weren't always one step behind."

As they continued walking, the forest began to thin, the dark, twisted trees giving way to the edge of the woods. Beyond the forest, they could see the distant silhouette of the Arcane Academy, its towering spires rising against the horizon. It should have felt like a haven after the dangers they had faced, but Ivy could not shake the feeling that something was terribly wrong.

The air around the Academy was different—heavier, as if the magic in the very atmosphere was distorted.

Rowan slowed, his eyes narrowing. "Do you feel that?"

Ivy nodded. "Something's happening at the Academy."

They quickened their pace, the weight of the Shadow King's lingering threat pressing on them. As they neared the Academy's gates, they saw students and professors gathered in the courtyard, their faces filled with confusion and fear. Whispers filled the air—rumors of strange events, magical disturbances, and dark forces at play.

Professor Aeliana, one of the Academy's senior instructors, approached them as they entered the courtyard. Her usually calm demeanor was strained, her eyes filled with worry.

"Where have you been?" she demanded; her voice sharp. "The Academy's wards have been breached. Dark magic is seeping into the grounds. The headmaster has gone missing."

Ivy's heart sank. "The headmaster? But... how?"

"We don't know," Professor Aeliana said, shaking her head. "The wards should have protected the Academy from any external threats, but they've been compromised. The magic feels... ancient. Dark. I fear it's connected to the Obsidian Forest."

Rowan's expression darkened. "The Shadow King."

Professor Aeliana's eyes widened. "The Shadow King? He is more than a myth?"

"He's real," Ivy said, her voice grim. "And he's after the Relic of Shadows."

A tense silence fell over them as the weight of Ivy's words sank in.

"Then we must find the headmaster and strengthen the wards," Professor Aeliana said, her voice firm. "The Academy cannot fall. If the Shadow King breaches these walls, we'll have nowhere left to hide."

Rowan nodded. "We'll help however we can, but we need to find the Relic first. It's the only way to stop the Shadow King for good."

Professor Aeliana hesitated, then sighed. "Very well. But be careful. The dark magic around the Academy is unlike anything I have felt before. It's growing stronger by the hour."

As the professor left to organize the defenses, Ivy, Rowan, and Aiden exchanged a glance. The situation was spiraling out of control, and they were running out of time.

Ivy unfolded the map again, studying the glowing runes. "The next clue should be somewhere near the Academy," she said, tracing the lines carefully. "But it's not clear were."

Suddenly, the runes shifted, glowing brighter as a new path appeared on the map. The lines curved toward the west, leading into the mountains that loomed beyond the Academy.

"The Relic is hidden in the mountains," Rowan said, his voice tense. "We need to get there before the Shadow King does."

Without hesitation, the trio set off, their determination renewed. The mountains ahead were treacherous, filled with ancient magic and forgotten dangers, but Ivy knew they had no choice.

As they approached the towering peaks, the air grew colder, and the sky darkened with thick, swirling clouds. A storm was brewing—one that would test not just their skills, but their very will to survive.

And in the shadows of the mountains, Ivy could feel it—the Relic of Shadows, pulsing with dark power, waiting for them to find it.

But so was the Shadow King.

The final battle was coming, and the fate of the Arcane Academy—and the world—hung in the balance.

Chapter 11: Trials of the Veil

The wind howled as Ivy, Rowan, and Aiden reached the foot of the mountains. The path ahead twisted upwards, carved into the rock by ancient hands. A thick fog clung to the cliffs, swirling ominously as though alive, obscuring the way forward. It was no ordinary mist—this was the Veil of Trials, a magical barrier that had protected the Relic of Shadows for centuries.

"Looks inviting," Aiden muttered, staring at the dense fog.

Rowan stepped forward; his wand raised. "The Veil is a test. Only those worthies of the Relic can pass through. If we're going to face the Shadow King, we have no choice."

Ivy nodded, though a knot of dread tightened in her stomach. They had faced many dangers on their journey so far, but the Veil was a test of mind and soul. It would prey on their deepest fears and desires, and there would be no way to know what awaited them on the other side.

As they approached the Veil, the fog seemed to shift, parting slightly to reveal a narrow path. The runes on the map glowed faintly, as if urging them forward.

"Stay close," Ivy said, gripping her wand tightly. "Whatever happens in there, we don't get separated."

With that, they stepped into the Veil.

The world around them instantly changed. The fog thickened, swallowing the mountains and the path they had come from. There was no sound, no wind, only an eerie silence. Ivy could feel the magic of the Veil pressing against her, whispering at the edges of her mind.

Suddenly, the fog parted before them, revealing three separate paths. Each one seemed identical, disappearing into the mist, but Ivy knew this was part of the trial. They were meant to choose.

"Which way?" Aiden asked, his voice uneasy.

Before Ivy could answer, the ground beneath their feet trembled, and ghostly figures appeared, materializing from the fog. They were not fully formed—more like shadows of the past—each one standing at the entrance of a different path.

Ivy's heart skipped a beat. These figures were familiar.

In front of the first path stood her mother, her face kind but filled with sorrow. In front of the second path, Aiden's brother appeared, a ghostly figure lost to the darkness long ago. The third figure was Rowan's mentor, a powerful wizard who had vanished under mysterious circumstances years before.

The figures did not speak, but their presence was enough to send chills down Ivy's spine. She knew these were not real—they were illusions, designed to lure them in—but the emotions they stirred were very real.

"It's a trick," Rowan said, his voice tight. "The Veil is trying to make us choose based on our past."

Aiden clenched his fists, his eyes locked on the figure of his brother. "But what if it's not? What if—?"

"It's not real," Ivy interrupted, though her own voice wavered. Her mother's face was so clear, so close, it hurt to look at her. "We can't give in."

Rowan took a deep breath, tearing his gaze away from his mentor. "The Veil tests your heart, your will. It wants to break us before we even reach the Relic."

As if to confirm his words, the ghostly figures began to move, stepping forward. They stretched out their hands, beckoning silently.

Ivy's mother's eyes glistened with unshed tears, her voice a whisper carried on the wind. "Come, Ivy. You're safe here with me."

Ivy's heart ached. Memories of her childhood, the warmth of her mother's arms, rushed back to her, threatening to overwhelm her resolve. She fought to stay grounded, reminding herself that this was an illusion. This was not real.

But the pull was strong. Too strong.

Aiden was already taking a step toward his brother's ghostly form, his expression one of desperate hope. "What if... what if we're wrong?" he whispered. "What if this is a chance to fix what we lost?"

Rowan grabbed Aiden's arm, stopping him. "No. This is the Veil. It's trying to trap us."

Ivy closed her eyes, forcing herself to focus. "We need to break the illusion."

She raised her wand, summoning all her strength. "Lumos Veritas!"

A brilliant light burst from her wand, cutting through the fog like a blade. The ghostly figures recoiled, their forms flickering as the light exposed them for what they truly were—shadows, fragments of magic designed to deceive.

The illusions shattered, dissolving into mist. The paths ahead cleared, revealing a single true path.

Ivy let out a breath she had not realized she was holding. "That was too close."

Rowan nodded, his face pale. "The Veil won't make this easy. We'll face more trials before we reach the Relic."

They continued down the path, the fog shifting around them once more. Ivy could feel the weight of the Veil pressing on them, growing stronger with each step. The next trial would not be as simple as illusions.

The path narrowed, and the fog thickened again, swirling faster until it formed a massive doorway made of shimmering light. Etched into the glowing archway were ancient runes, symbols Ivy recognized from her studies. The Trial of the Veil had another stage.

"The Runes of Insight," Rowan murmured, his eyes scanning the symbols. "We have to solve the puzzle to pass through."

Aiden frowned. "And if we fail?"

"The Veil will trap us here forever," Ivy said softly.

No pressure, she thought grimly.

The runes began to glow brighter, shifting and rearranging themselves into a pattern that pulsed with energy. Ivy could feel the magic humming in the air, the weight of the Veil pressing down harder than before.

Each of them took a step forward, studying the runes. The solution was not immediately obvious, but Ivy could sense that the answer lay in something deeper than simple logic. The Veil tested their hearts and minds, not just their knowledge.

"Look," Aiden said suddenly, pointing to one of the runes. "It's changing with our thoughts."

Ivy focused on the runes, willing them to reveal their secret. The runes flickered, responding to her magic. Then it hit her—the runes reflected their fears, their doubts. To pass through, they would need to confront their inner turmoil.

"Clear your mind," Ivy whispered, stepping forward. "Don't let fear control you."

As they concentrated, the runes began to shift and align, each of them silently pushing past their own fears. The doorway pulsed once, then opened, revealing the final stretch of the path.

They had passed the trial.

But Ivy knew this was only the beginning. The Veil had tested them, but the real challenge lay ahead. The Relic of Shadows waited, and with it, the final confrontation with the Shadow King.

There was no turning back now.

Chapter 12: The Forgotten Ritual

As Ivy, Rowan, and Aiden stepped through the shimmering doorway, the air grew colder, and the atmosphere shifted. The Veil of Trials was behind them, but they could sense the presence of something ancient and powerful ahead. The path wound deeper into the mountains, leading to a hidden valley where the Ritual of Shadows was said to have been performed long ago.

"This place... it feels different," Rowan muttered, his breath fogging in the cold air.

Ivy nodded; her senses heightened. The valley ahead was silent, but it thrummed with a dormant power. They were entering the heart of the ancient magic that had once bound the Shadow King and hidden the Relic of Shadows.

Aiden glanced around nervously. "I thought the trials were supposed to be over. Why does it feel like we are walking into another trap?"

"Because we might be," Ivy replied, her voice low. "The Ritual was forgotten for a reason. If the Shadow King wants the Relic, it means the magic here is still active—dangerous."

They descended into the valley, their footsteps crunching against the frost-covered ground. In the distance, a ruined temple came into view, its once-majestic columns now crumbling, overtaken by nature. The temple's design was unmistakably ancient, its stone walls etched with the same runes they had seen on the Veil. Vines twisted through the cracks, and dark clouds loomed overhead, casting long shadows across the ground.

At the center of the temple stood an altar, its surface worn from centuries of exposure but still pulsing with a faint magical glow. Ivy could feel the weight of the magic in the air, a remnant of the Ritual that had taken place here so long ago.

"This is it," Ivy whispered. "The Ritual of Shadows."

Rowan stepped forward cautiously, his eyes scanning the ruins. "We need to find out how it works. If the Ritual was used to bind the Shadow King once, maybe it can stop him again."

Ivy approached the altar, running her fingers over the runes carved into the stone. The markings were worn, but she could make out fragments of a spell, ancient words of power that she could barely comprehend. As she traced the lines, a vision flickered in her mind—an image of hooded figures performing the Ritual under a blood-red sky, their voices chanting in unison as dark magic swirled around them.

Suddenly, the ground trembled, and the runes on the altar began to glow. The ancient magic was awakening.

Aiden stepped back, alarmed. "Uh, guys? I think we just triggered something."

Before they could react, the sky above them darkened, and a low, ominous hum filled the air. The magic surrounding the temple was coming to life, responding to their presence. The air grew thick with energy, and the shadows around them began to shift and move, coalescing into dark, ethereal forms.

"Shadows," Rowan warned, raising his wand. "They're drawn to the magic of the Ritual."

The shadowy figures closed in, their forms flickering and formless, like living darkness. Ivy felt the weight of their gaze, a cold, suffocating presence that threatened to overwhelm her.

"We have to finish the Ritual," Ivy shouted over the rising wind. "It's the only way to stop them!"

Rowan and Aiden nodded, their wands raised, ready to defend against the encroaching shadows. Ivy turned her attention back to the altar, her mind racing. She needed to complete the spell—the same one the ancient wizards had used—but the words were incomplete, fragmented by time.

Suddenly, a voice echoed in her mind, faint and distant, as if it were coming from the past. It was the voice of the Ritual itself, guiding her.

"To bind the darkness, one must offer light. To seal the shadows, a sacrifice of the purest magic."

Ivy's heart raced. The Ritual required a sacrifice—a powerful one. But what kind of magic could seal away the Shadow King?

"The Relic," Rowan said, as if reading her thoughts. "It's the key. The Relic of Shadows can complete the Ritual."

"But we don't have it yet!" Aiden shouted, fending off a shadow that had gotten too close.

Ivy's mind worked furiously. The Relic might be hidden, but they had something just as powerful—the Heart of Aether, the artifact they had recovered from the Obsidian Forest. It pulsed with ancient energy, a source of pure magic that could rival the darkness of the Relic.

She pulled the Heart from her cloak, its light glowing bright against the encroaching shadows. The moment it touched the altar, the runes flared to life, and the shadows around them recoiled, hissing as the light drove them back.

"It's working!" Ivy cried; her voice strained as she channeled her magic into the Heart. The light grew stronger, illuminating the entire temple.

But the shadows were not giving up so easily. They surged forward, a mass of darkness intent on stopping the Ritual. Rowan and Aiden stood their ground, their wands blazing with spells as they fought to hold the line.

"Keep going, Ivy!" Rowan called out, blasting a shadow into the air. "We've got this!"

THE ARCANE ACADEMY - THE SHATTERED VEIL

Ivy focused all her energy on the altar, the words of the ancient spell forming in her mind. The magic surged through her, a powerful force that seemed to connect her to the very fabric of the Ritual. The Heart of Aether pulsed in time with her heartbeat, growing brighter and brighter.

"By light, I bind thee. By magic, I seal thee. By the power of Aether, I banish the shadows!"

With a final surge of energy, the light exploded from the Heart, bathing the entire valley in a brilliant glow. The shadows let out an anguished wail as they were consumed by the light, their forms dissolving into nothingness.

The wind died down, and the magic around them began to fade. The temple was silent once more, the shadows banished.

Ivy collapsed to her knees, exhausted but relieved. The Ritual was complete.

Rowan and Aiden hurried to her side, helping her to her feet.

"You did it," Rowan said, his voice filled with awe.

Ivy nodded, still catching her breath. "We did it. But this is not over. The Shadow King will know we have performed the Ritual. He'll be coming for us—and the Relic."

Aiden glanced around warily. "Then we need to find it before he does."

As they prepared to leave the temple, Ivy could not shake the feeling that something had changed. The Ritual had awakened an ancient power, one that was tied not just to the Relic of Shadows, but to the very magic that governed their world and she had a sinking feeling that the Shadow King was already one step ahead.

They needed to find the Relic—and fast.

Time was running out.

Chapter 13: Secrets of the Academy

The halls of Arcane Academy felt different in the wake of the forgotten Ritual's completion. Ivy, Rowan, and Aiden returned to the school; their minds heavy with the knowledge that the Shadow King was closer to reclaiming his power. But it was not just the looming darkness that weighed on them; the Academy itself seemed to be hiding secrets of its own.

"I can't shake the feeling that we're missing something," Ivy said as they walked through the grand corridors, her eyes darting to the shadowy corners. "The Academy—there's something it hasn't told us."

"You're right," Rowan agreed, keeping his voice low. "Everything we've uncovered points back here. The Relic, the Ritual, even the Shadow King... it all seems connected to this place."

Aiden frowned, glancing over his shoulder as if someone was listening. "But how? The Academy was built centuries after the Relic was hidden, wasn't it?"

Ivy paused, her gaze landing on one of the many ornate tapestries that lined the walls of the school. Each one depicted an important moment in magical history, but now, she saw them in a different light. There were hidden layers to the Academy's past—layers they had not yet uncovered.

"It's time we start looking deeper," she said with conviction.

That night, the trio gathered in the quiet confines of the library. It was the largest and oldest part of the Academy, housing thousands of ancient texts—many of which were strictly off-limits to students. The forbidden section loomed in the back; its towering iron gates locked with wards only professors were allowed to access.

"We've tried searching the public records," Ivy said, her voice barely a whisper as they huddled together at a dusty table. "But the real answers are likely hidden where no one's allowed to go."

"The forbidden section," Rowan said, glancing toward the gate.

Aiden gave a low whistle. "Are you sure about this? We could get expelled just for thinking about it."

"We don't have a choice," Ivy replied, her determination unshakable. "If we're going to stop the Shadow King, we need to know what the Academy is hiding."

Using the knowledge they had gained from the Ritual; Ivy crafted a spell to break through the wards. As they waited for the perfect moment, the midnight chimes echoed through the empty halls. The school was asleep, and now was their chance.

With a single flick of her wand, Ivy murmured the incantation. The wards surrounding the gate shimmered, resisting for a moment before dissolving into thin air. The iron gates creaked open, revealing rows upon rows of forbidden knowledge.

They stepped into the forbidden section, the air immediately colder and thicker with magic. Ancient tomes lined the shelves, their pages yellowed with age. Some of the books seemed to hum with dark energy, while others were sealed with locks that pulsed with magic.

"We need to find something about the Academy's origins," Ivy whispered, her voice reverberating through the eerie silence. "Anything that connects the school to the Relic or the Shadow King."

They split up, each diving into the ancient texts. Ivy pulled out an old leather-bound book marked with a symbol she recognized from the temple where they had performed the Ritual. Rowan and Aiden combed through scrolls and parchments, their faces tense with concentration.

As Ivy flipped through the brittle pages, her heart skipped a beat. There, in the middle of the book, was an entry about the founding of Arcane Academy—yet it was not the story she had learned in her history lessons.

The Academy had been built not just as a place of learning, but as a safeguard. It was designed to protect something ancient, something dangerous.

"The Academy wasn't just a school," Ivy whispered, her eyes widening. "It was created to hide the Relic."

Rowan looked up from his scrolls, stunned. "Are you sure?"

Ivy nodded, pointing to the passage. "It's all here. The founders knew about the Relic of Shadows and feared what would happen if it ever fell into the wrong hands. They built the Academy as a fortress to protect it."

Aiden frowned. "But that means the Relic is here, in the Academy."

Ivy's mind raced. The Relic they had been searching for was not hidden in some far-off, dangerous location—it was within the very walls of the Academy. All along, they had been walking through the halls of a fortress designed to keep the Shadow King from ever reclaiming his power.

But if the Academy had been built to protect the Relic, why hadn't they been told? Why had the truth been buried?

Suddenly, a creaking sound echoed through the forbidden section. The trio froze, their hearts pounding.

"Someone's coming," Rowan whispered.

They quickly extinguished their wands and ducked behind a row of shelves, their breath shallow as footsteps approached. The heavy clack of boots on stone echoed louder and louder, drawing closer to their hiding spot.

Ivy held her breath, her mind racing. Who could it be? A professor? The headmaster? Or someone worse?

THE ARCANE ACADEMY - THE SHATTERED VEIL

The footsteps stopped just outside their hiding place. A figure draped in dark robes appeared, their face obscured by a hood. The figure paused, scanning the forbidden section, as if searching for something—or someone.

Ivy's heart pounded in her chest. Whoever this was, they were not here by accident. Could they know about the Relic too?

The figure lingered for a moment longer before turning and disappearing into the shadows, leaving the trio trembling with adrenaline.

As soon as the figure was gone, they emerged from their hiding spot, hearts still racing.

"We need to get out of here," Aiden whispered urgently. "Now."

But Ivy was already thinking ahead. The Academy was hiding the Relic, and now they knew the truth. The only question that remained was how to find it—and who else was searching for it.

Because if they did not find it soon, someone else would.

And the Shadow King was not the only danger lurking in the halls of the Arcane Academy.

Chapter 14: The Betrayal

The weight of the truth hung heavy over the trio. They had uncovered too much, learned too many dark secrets about Arcane Academy to simply return to their routines. Ivy's heart raced with unease. The Academy—once a place of learning and safety—now felt like a web of lies, and she could not shake the feeling that someone close to them was hiding even more.

As the days passed, Ivy, Rowan, and Aiden dove deeper into their search for the Relic, sneaking into hidden chambers and poring over forbidden texts. The closer they got to the truth, the more dangerous their situation became. Professors started watching them with suspicion, and whispers followed them through the halls. It was clear that not everyone wanted the truth to be revealed.

One evening, as the group gathered in an abandoned classroom to piece together their findings, Rowan looked up from the ancient map he was studying and spoke in a hushed voice. "There's something we're missing. The Academy's founders created this place to hide the Relic, but I don't think they were the only ones who knew about it."

Ivy furrowed her brow, her fingers tracing a line on the map. "You think someone else is involved? Someone inside the Academy?"

Before Rowan could answer, the door to the classroom creaked open. Startled, they quickly hid the map and turned to see who had entered. A figure stepped into the dim light—it was Professor Damaris, one of the most respected and trusted instructors at the Academy. Her usual calm demeanor was replaced by an icy glare.

"You've been meddling where you don't belong," she said, her voice low but filled with menace. "I warned you all to stay away from the forbidden knowledge, but you didn't listen."

Ivy's heart pounded in her chest. "Professor, we—"

"Silence!" Damaris snapped; her eyes blazing. "You have no idea the danger you're putting yourselves in. The Relic is not a treasure to be found—it is a curse that must remain hidden."

Aiden stepped forward, his voice firm. "If the Relic is so dangerous, why hasn't anyone told us the truth? Why keep it a secret?"

Damaris's expression softened for a moment, as if she was torn between her duty and something deeper. But then her face hardened again. "Because it is the only way to protect the world from the Shadow King. You think you're helping, but all you're doing is hastening his return."

Rowan shook his head. "No, we're trying to stop him. We just need to understand how."

The professor sighed heavily; her eyes filled with regret. "I wish I could help you, but it's too late. You've gone too far."

Before they could react, the door burst open again, and a group of Academy guards stormed in, their wands raised and glowing with magical energy. Ivy's heart sank as she realized what was happening. They had been betrayed.

"Take them," Damaris ordered, her voice cold and final. "They know too much."

In a flash, the guards surged forward, and the trio barely had time to draw their wands before they were surrounded. Ivy could feel the power of the binding spell wrapping around her, making it impossible to move. Panic set in as she struggled against the magic holding her in place.

"I trusted you!" Ivy shouted at Damaris, her voice filled with hurt and betrayal.

Damaris's expression faltered for a moment, a flicker of sadness crossing her face. "You don't understand, Ivy. I'm doing this to protect you—before you become a pawn in a game much larger than you can imagine."

With that, the guards led Ivy, Rowan, and Aiden away, their fates now in the hands of those who had kept the Academy's darkest secrets hidden for centuries.

As they were dragged through the halls of the Academy, Ivy's mind raced. They had been so close to finding the Relic, to uncovering the truth. But now, they were prisoners, betrayed by someone they had trusted. And worse, they had no idea who else in the Academy was involved—or how deep the betrayal truly ran.

But one thing was certain: the Shadow King's return was no longer a distant threat. It was happening, and time was running out.

Chapter 15: The Gathering Storm

The dungeon beneath Arcane Academy was nothing like Ivy had imagined. Cold, damp, and eerily silent, it was a stark contrast to the grandeur above. Ivy, Rowan, and Aiden sat shackled in a small, dimly lit cell; their magical powers suppressed by the iron cuffs on their wrists. The betrayal by Professor Damaris still stung, but there was no time to dwell on it. They were running out of time, and the storm was coming.

"What do we do now?" Aiden asked, his voice barely above a whisper. His face was pale in the low light, his eyes wide with fear.

Rowan, leaning against the stone wall, clenched his fists. "We can't stay here. The Relic is still out there, and the Shadow King is gaining strength. We need to get out of here and stop him before it's too late."

Ivy, though shaken by their capture, felt a growing determination stir within her. The betrayal had shaken her to her core, but it had also ignited a fire. "We've come too far to give up now," she said firmly. "There has to be a way out of here."

Before any of them could respond, the door to the dungeon creaked open. A figure stepped through the shadows, hooded, and cloaked. The trio tensed, expecting the worst, but as the figure drew closer, Ivy's breath caught in her throat.

It was Lysandra, the enigmatic rogue mage who had helped them before. Her silver eyes gleamed in the faint torchlight, and without a word, she flicked her wrist, sending a wave of magic through the air.

The iron cuffs around their wrists shattered with a metallic clang, and Ivy felt the familiar surge of her magic return.

"Didn't expect to see me again, did you?" Lysandra smirked, pulling back her hood.

"Lysandra," Rowan breathed in relief, "how did you—?"

"There's no time for that," Lysandra interrupted. "I heard about what happened, and I couldn't leave you to rot down here. The Academy is hiding more than just the Relic. Things are far worse than you know."

"How much worse?" Ivy asked, already dreading the answer.

Lysandra's face grew grim. "The Shadow King's forces are already on the move. His followers are gathering in secret, even here in the Academy. And they're not just looking for the Relic—they're planning to open the Rift."

Ivy felt a chill run down her spine. The Rift—the ancient tear between their world and the dark realm of the Shadow King. If it was opened, the Shadow King would not just regain his powers. He would invade their world, unleashing destruction like never before.

"That's impossible," Aiden said, his voice trembling. "The Rift has been sealed for centuries. No one can open it."

"Not unless they have the right magic," Lysandra said darkly. "And the Relic is the key."

Rowan stood up; his jaw clenched. "We have to stop them. But first, we need to find the Relic before they do."

Lysandra nodded. "I can help you, but we have to move quickly. The storm is coming, and when it hits, the Academy will not be safe anymore. There are enemies within these walls, waiting for the right moment to strike."

As they made their way out of the dungeon, Ivy's mind raced. Everything was falling apart faster than they had imagined. The Shadow King's influence was spreading, even inside the Academy, and their list of allies was growing thinner by the day.

They emerged into the darkened corridors of the Academy, the stone walls seeming to pulse with a strange energy. Outside, the sky had turned an ominous shade of gray, swirling with clouds that crackled with distant thunder. A magical storm was brewing—not just in the heavens, but in the heart of the Academy itself.

"We need to reach the Vault," Lysandra whispered urgently. "That's where the Relic has been hidden all these years."

"The Vault?" Ivy asked, keeping her voice low. "Where is it?"

"Deep beneath the Academy," Lysandra replied. "It's guarded by ancient wards, magic stronger than anything you've encountered. But if we can bypass them, we'll find the Relic before the Shadow King's followers do."

As they made their way through the twisting passageways, Ivy could not help but feel the weight of everything they had learned. The Academy—once a place of safety and knowledge—was crumbling under the weight of its own secrets. And now, the very students and professors they had trusted were preparing for the return of the greatest evil their world had ever known.

They reached the entrance to the Vault, a massive stone door etched with glowing runes. Lysandra stepped forward, her hand hovering over the symbols. "This will take everything I've got," she muttered. "The wards are ancient, and they won't go down easily."

"Do it," Rowan urged, his eyes scanning the corridor for any sign of trouble.

As Lysandra began chanting, her voice low and steady, the runes on the door flared to life, pulsing with ancient power. Ivy held her breath, feeling the magic in the air grow heavy. The storm outside was growing fiercer, the thunder now shaking the very walls of the Academy.

Finally, with a blinding flash of light, the wards shattered, and the stone door groaned open.

Inside, the Vault was cold and dark, its walls lined with shelves holding magical artifacts of untold power. But in the center of the room, resting on a pedestal of obsidian, was the Relic of Shadows. It was small, barely the size of a fist, but it radiated an overwhelming sense of power—both dark and ancient.

"We've found it," Aiden whispered, his eyes wide.

But before they could take another step, a chilling voice echoed through the Vault.

"You're too late."

From the shadows emerged Professor Damaris, her eyes glowing with malevolent energy. Behind her, a group of shadowy figures—followers of the Shadow King—stepped forward, their wands raised.

Ivy's heart sank. The storm had arrived.

"You should have stayed in the dungeon," Damaris sneered, her voice cold and deadly. "Now, the Relic will be ours. And with it, we will open the Rift."

The room crackled with dark magic, the storm outside reaching its peak. Ivy, Rowan, Aiden, and Lysandra stood frozen, knowing that the battle for the Relic—and the fate of their world—was about to begin.

The storm had gathered. Now, they would have to survive it.

Chapter 16: The Heart of the Veil

The air inside the Vault crackled with tension. The Relic of Shadows sat ominously on the pedestal, its dark aura pulsing like a heartbeat, casting flickering shadows across the stone chamber. Ivy, Rowan, Aiden, and Lysandra stood on one side, while Professor Damaris and the Shadow King's followers blocked their path to the Relic.

"Step aside," Damaris commanded, her voice sharp with authority. "You do not know the forces you are dealing with. The Relic belongs to us, and with it, the Rift will be opened."

Ivy's heart pounded in her chest. She could feel the storm raging outside, shaking the foundations of the Academy. The power inside the Vault was overwhelming, but she could not let the Shadow King's followers win. They had come too far to fail now.

Rowan stepped forward; his wand drawn. "We will not let you take the Relic. This ends here, Damaris."

The professor's lips curled into a cold smile. "You are brave, but foolish. You still do not understand, do you? The Shadow King's return is inevitable. And once the Rift is open, his power will consume everything. No one can stop it."

Lysandra narrowed her eyes, stepping up beside Rowan. "We'll see about that."

With a flick of her wrist, Lysandra unleashed a burst of magic that sent a shockwave through the Vault. The followers of the Shadow

King scattered, raising their wands in defense as the room erupted into chaos. Sparks of magic flew in every direction, illuminating the darkness as spells collided midair.

Ivy, her heart racing, focused on the Relic. It was the key to everything—the source of the Shadow King's power, and possibly the only way to stop him. She had to reach it before Damaris or the others did.

"We need to get to the Relic!" Ivy shouted over the roar of magic. "It's the only way!"

Aiden nodded, his face pale but determined. "I'll cover you."

With a surge of adrenaline, Ivy darted toward the pedestal, ducking beneath a barrage of dark spells. She could feel the Relic's power pulling her in, a magnetic force that both repelled and beckoned her. It was as if the object itself was alive, aware of their presence.

But just as she reached the pedestal, Damaris appeared in a flash of dark energy, blocking her path.

"You're too late, Ivy," Damaris hissed, her eyes glowing with dark magic. "You are out of your depth. The Relic is not something you can control."

Ivy's pulse quickened. "I don't need to control it—I just need to keep it out of your hands."

With that, Ivy raised her wand, summoning every ounce of magic she had. A brilliant light burst from her wand, slamming into Damaris with enough force to send the professor stumbling back. But Damaris recovered quickly, her own wand crackling with dark energy.

"You've made a mistake, child," Damaris growled. "You should have stayed hidden."

Before Ivy could react, Damaris unleashed a wave of dark magic that knocked her off her feet. The force of the spell sent her crashing into the stone floor, pain shooting through her body.

"Ivy!" Rowan shouted; his voice filled with panic.

As Ivy struggled to her feet, her vision blurred, she saw the Relic pulsing brighter, its power filling the room. It was reacting to the magic around it—feeding off the battle, growing stronger with every spell cast.

And then, something strange happened.

The air in the Vault shimmered, and the room seemed to shift. Ivy blinked, her breath catching in her throat as she realized what was happening. The veil between worlds—the barrier that kept the Shadow King's realm from theirs—was thinning. The Relic's power was tearing it apart.

"The Rift!" Lysandra shouted; her voice strained with effort as she battled the Shadow King's followers. "The Relic is opening the Rift!"

Ivy's heart raced. If the Rift opened completely, the Shadow King would return, and their world would be lost. She could not let that happen.

Summoning every bit of strength she had, Ivy pushed herself to her feet and ran toward the Relic. Damaris was distracted, her attention focused on battling Rowan and Aiden. This was Ivy's chance.

With a final burst of magic, Ivy reached the pedestal and grabbed the Relic.

The moment her fingers closed around it, a surge of energy shot through her, overwhelming her senses. The Relic's power was unlike anything she had ever felt before—dark, ancient, and terrifyingly powerful. It whispered to her, tempting her with promises of unimaginable strength.

But Ivy knew better. The Relic was dangerous, and its power came at a cost.

Clenching her jaw, she focused on the one thing that mattered: closing the Rift.

With the Relic in her hand, Ivy raised her wand and called upon the magic within her. The Vault trembled as her spell clashed with the

Relic's power, the very air vibrating with the force of the magic. It felt like the world was tearing apart at the seams.

But slowly, agonizingly, the Rift began to close.

Damaris, realizing what was happening, let out a furious scream. "No! You cannot stop it! The Shadow King will rise!"

Ivy's body trembled with exhaustion, but she did not stop. She could not stop. The Relic's power surged through her, threatening to consume her, but she held on, focusing all her magic on sealing the Rift.

And then, with a deafening crack, the Rift closed.

The Vault fell silent.

Ivy collapsed to the ground, the Relic slipping from her hand. Her vision blurred, and the last thing she saw before darkness claimed her was the faint glow of the Relic, its power fading as the veil between worlds sealed once more.

The storm had passed, but the danger was far from over.

Chapter 17: The Shattered Alliance

The corridors of Arcane Academy were eerily quiet as Ivy awoke in the infirmary, her body aching from the strain of the battle. The memories of the Vault, the Relic, and the closing Rift rushed back, bringing with them a mix of relief and dread. She had stopped the Rift from opening, but something about the moment still haunted her—an ominous feeling that the battle was far from over.

"Ivy," a voice called softly.

She turned to see Rowan standing beside her bed, his expression tense but relieved. Aiden sat on a nearby chair, arms crossed, staring at the floor, while Lysandra stood in the corner, her face shadowed by the low light of the room.

"You did it," Rowan said, his voice quiet but full of pride. "You closed the Rift."

Ivy shook her head, her mind racing. "But Damaris... She escaped, didn't she?"

Rowan's face darkened. "Yes, she did. Her and the rest of the Shadow King's followers vanished as soon as the Rift was sealed. We have been searching for them, but they are hiding somewhere. And the worst part is... the Academy is divided."

Ivy's heart sank. "What do you mean?"

Aiden spoke up, his voice low and bitter. "After what happened, not everyone believes the Academy should keep resisting the Shadow

King. Some of the professors and students think we should align with him—they believe Damaris was right."

Ivy's blood ran cold. "They're siding with the Shadow King?"

Rowan nodded grimly. "There are whispers throughout the halls. People are scared, and Damaris sowed enough doubt to make them question everything. Some think it is safer to join him, to accept the inevitable."

Lysandra stepped forward; her silver eyes sharp. "We are running out of time. The Academy is on the brink of civil war. If we do not act fast, Damaris and her followers will use the chaos to their advantage. They will strike when we are weakest."

Ivy sat up, wincing from the lingering pain in her body. "We cannot let that happen. We need to find Damaris and stop her before she can regroup. She is still after the Relic, and if she finds it again..."

"The Shadow King will rise," Aiden finished, his voice filled with grim resolve.

Rowan sat beside Ivy; his eyes filled with worry. "It is worse than that. The Relic—it is connected to the heart of the Academy itself. There is a hidden power here, something ancient and dangerous, and Damaris knows it. She is not just after the Relic anymore. She is after whatever is buried deep beneath Arcane Academy."

Ivy's mind whirled with the implications. The Academy had always been a place of mystery, with secrets hidden in every corner. But this was something else. If there was a power beneath the school that Damaris could use to awaken the Shadow King, the stakes were higher than they had ever imagined.

"We need to unite the Academy," Ivy said firmly, her voice stronger than she felt. "We need to show everyone that the Shadow King is the real threat, not the answer."

"How?" Aiden asked, shaking his head. "People are scared. They are losing faith. They will follow whoever promises them safety—even if that means siding with Damaris."

Lysandra crossed her arms, her eyes narrowing in thought. "The only way to do that is to expose Damaris for what she really is. If we can reveal her plans, show the Academy that she is working with the Shadow King to destroy everything we know, we might be able to break her influence."

Rowan stood, determination in his eyes. "Then we need to find proof. Damaris and her followers are hiding somewhere in the Academy—we just need to find them."

"And when we do," Ivy said, her voice steady, "we end this once and for all."

The group exchanged tense looks, knowing what lay ahead. The Academy was fractured, their allies few, and the storm that had passed was only the beginning.

They moved quickly, searching through ancient records and hidden passages within the Academy's vast and winding structure. As the hours passed, the atmosphere grew tenser. The whispers of betrayal grew louder, and Ivy could feel the divide widening among the students and staff. Once united in their purpose, the Academy now felt like a battleground, with every glance filled with suspicion.

It was not long before they found their lead.

Lysandra, her skills as a rogue mage invaluable, had uncovered an encrypted message in the headmaster's chambers. It pointed to an abandoned wing of the Academy; a place long forgotten by most—The Heart of the Veil.

"The Heart of the Veil," Rowan whispered as they gathered around the old map. "I have heard of it. It is supposed to be the source of the Academy's magic, the place where the lines between worlds are thinnest."

"That's where Damaris is hiding," Lysandra said, her eyes gleaming with certainty. "And if she's there, she's planning something big."

Aiden frowned; his brow furrowed in worry. "If we confront her there, we'll be walking right into her trap."

"I know," Ivy said, her voice quiet but determined. "But we do not have a choice. This is the only way to stop her."

With the plan set, the group made their way toward the Heart of the Veil. The once-grand hallways of the Academy seemed darker, the air heavy with the weight of the betrayal that had torn the school apart. Ivy could feel the magic in the air, thick and charged with anticipation. The storm was about to break, and this time, there would be no turning back.

As they descended deeper into the abandoned wing, the shadows grew longer, and the temperature dropped. The very walls seemed to hum with ancient power, a reminder of the forces they were about to face. And then, in the distance, they saw it—a flickering light, casting long shadows across the floor.

Ivy's heart pounded in her chest as they approached. The flickering light grew stronger, and soon, they found themselves standing before a vast chamber—the Heart of the Veil.

Damaris stood in the center, her eyes glowing with dark magic. Around her, the Shadow King's followers chanted in an ancient, forgotten tongue. The air was thick with power, the veil between worlds dangerously thin.

"You're too late," Damaris sneered, her voice echoing through the chamber. "The Academy will fall, and with it, the veil will shatter. The Shadow King will rise."

Ivy stepped forward, her wand at the ready. "Not if we stop you first."

With a flick of her wrist, Damaris unleashed a wave of dark magic. The ground shook, and the very fabric of reality seemed to twist and warp around them. The battle for the Heart of the Veil—and the fate of the Academy—had begun.

And Ivy knew, in the depths of her heart, that nothing would ever be the same.

Chapter 18: A World in Peril

The Heart of the Veil pulsed with dark magic, its energy thrumming through the chamber as Ivy and her companions braced themselves against the power radiating from Damaris. The ancient chamber, once a source of the Academy's magic, was now twisted into a battleground where reality itself seemed to warp and shudder. Shadows danced on the walls, cast by the ethereal glow of the Rift forming in the center.

"You can't stop it!" Damaris's voice rang through the cavernous space. Her eyes burned with dark fire, and her aura surged with the overwhelming power of the Shadow King. "The Veil is already tearing. When it breaks, the Shadow King will rise, and the world will belong to him!"

Ivy felt the weight of Damaris's words deep in her chest, but she could not give in to the fear clawing at her. She had faced worse odds before, but never had so much been at stake. All around her, the Veil—the barrier between their world and the Shadow Realm—was beginning to crack.

"We need to sever her connection to the Veil," Lysandra said, her voice urgent. She gripped her dagger tightly, eyes scanning the area for any weak point in Damaris's ritual. "If she completes it, the Rift will open fully."

Rowan took a step forward, his wand drawn, power crackling at his fingertips. "Then let's finish this before she does."

Without another word, the battle erupted. Rowan and Aiden hurled spell after spell, their magic colliding with Damaris's dark energy in bursts of light and shadow. The air crackled with power, and the ground trembled beneath their feet. Ivy darted between the chaotic blasts, searching for an opening. Damaris, however, moved with terrifying precision, deflecting every spell with ease, her dark magic feeding off the Rift's growing energy.

Lysandra disappeared into the shadows; her rogue skills honed to perfection. She circled the chamber, her eyes locked on Damaris, waiting for the moment to strike.

"Fools," Damaris spat, her voice dripping with disdain. "You think you can fight the inevitable? The Shadow King's return cannot be stopped!"

As if in response to her words, the Rift at the center of the room began to widen. A swirling vortex of black and violet energy spun wildly, and through its depths, Ivy could glimpse a dark, twisted world beyond—one where nightmares roamed freely, and the laws of their reality no longer held sway.

"We need to close that Rift!" Ivy shouted over the roar of the battle.

"I'm trying!" Rowan called back, sweat beading on his forehead as he pushed his magic to its limits. "But the energy...it's too strong."

Aiden, his face set in grim determination, summoned a wall of fire to block one of Damaris's dark spells, but the flames flickered and died almost instantly, snuffed out by the overwhelming power of the Rift. "We're running out of time!"

Ivy's heart pounded as she watched the Rift grow larger. The Veil was tearing apart, and if they did not stop it soon, everything they knew would be consumed by the Shadow King's realm. Desperation gnawed at her, but she forced herself to think. There had to be a way to stop this, to sever Damaris's connection to the Veil and close the Rift for good.

Then it hit her—the Relic.

The ancient artifact had been the key to closing the Rift before. Perhaps it could do the same again, but they needed to act fast before the Veil shattered completely.

"I have an idea," Ivy said, her voice steady despite the chaos around her. "We need to use the Relic!"

Rowan's eyes widened. "But it is unstable. If we try to tap into its power now—"

"We don't have a choice!" Ivy interrupted. "It's the only thing strong enough to stop this."

Rowan hesitated, but a glance at the Rift convinced him. "Fine. We will need to amplify its power—combine our magic with it. But if this backfire's..."

"We'll all be lost," Ivy finished grimly. "But it's a risk we have to take."

With no time to lose, Ivy reached into her satchel and pulled out the Relic. It pulsed with a faint, eerie glow, and as she held it up, she could feel its power resonating with the magic of the Veil. It was like holding a fragment of the universe in her hands—ancient, infinite, and dangerous.

Rowan, Aiden, and Lysandra gathered around her, their expressions a mix of determination and fear. Together, they focused their magic, channeling it through the Relic. The artifact glowed brighter, its energy swelling as it drew in their combined power. The air around them shimmered with raw magic, and the ground trembled under the weight of the energy they were unleashing.

Damaris's eyes widened as she realized what they were doing. "No!" she screamed; her voice filled with fury. "You won't take this from me!"

With a surge of dark magic, she hurled a massive blast toward them, but it was too late. The Relic flared with blinding light, and the energy it released shot toward the Rift, colliding with the dark magic tearing at the Veil.

For a moment, the entire world seemed to hang in the balance. The Relic's power pushed against the Rift, and for a heartbeat, Ivy thought they might fail. But then, with a deafening crack, the Rift began to shrink. The dark energy twisted and writhed, but the Relic's light was too strong.

The Veil began to mend.

Damaris screamed in rage, her connection to the Rift severed, her dark power waning. "No! This cannot be happening!" She raised her hands to cast another spell, but before she could, Lysandra moved like a shadow, her dagger flashing in the dim light. In one swift motion, she disarmed Damaris, sending her wand clattering to the ground.

"Your reign ends here," Lysandra said coldly.

Damaris glared at them, her eyes blazing with hatred. "You think you have won? The Shadow King will still rise. This world is already doomed!"

The Rift sealed with a final burst of light, and silence fell over the chamber. The Veil had held.

Ivy, exhausted but triumphant, lowered the Relic, its glow fading as the danger passed. The world had been saved—for now.

But as she looked at the trembling form of Damaris, bound by Lysandra's magic, Ivy could not shake the feeling that this was only the beginning. The Shadow King was still out there, waiting, watching, and the battle for their world was far from over.

A world in peril, but one that still had a fighting chance.

Chapter 19: The Final Ritual

The eerie silence in the chamber was suffocating. The once-vibrant air that pulsed with magical energy now felt still, as if the very fabric of the world was holding its breath. Ivy, Rowan, Aiden, and Lysandra stood at the heart of the ancient temple, staring down at the ornate altar that had been the centerpiece of countless rituals throughout history.

In their hands was the key to everything—the final piece of the puzzle that had eluded them for so long: *The Scroll of Eternum*. The ancient text contained the instructions for the only ritual powerful enough to destroy the Shadow King once and for all. But the ritual was as dangerous as it was powerful. The slightest mistake could unleash a force that would tear the world apart, leaving it vulnerable to the shadows forever.

"This is it," Ivy said, her voice barely more than a whisper. She could feel the weight of the scroll in her hands, its ancient parchment humming with latent power. "If we get this wrong…"

"We won't get it wrong," Rowan interrupted, his eyes fierce with determination. "We've come too far to fail now."

Aiden, ever the skeptic, crossed his arms and glanced warily at the darkened corners of the temple. "Are we sure this is the right place? The final ritual must be performed at the exact location the Veil was first created. If we are even slightly off…"

Lysandra, always calm in the face of danger, nodded toward the massive runes carved into the stone floor beneath them. "This is the place. The runes match the ones in the scroll. This temple was built for this purpose."

Ivy took a deep breath, steadying herself. The ritual required all their magic, their strength, and their will. It would push them beyond their limits. And even then, the outcome was uncertain.

As they prepared to begin, the ground trembled beneath their feet. The air grew colder, and a low rumble echoed from deep within the earth. Ivy's heart raced. They were running out of time. The Shadow King's forces were closing in, and soon, they would have to face the full might of the darkness.

"There's no going back now," Rowan said, stepping toward the altar. He unfurled the Scroll of Eternum, its ancient symbols glowing faintly in the dim light. "We begin."

The four of them stood around the altar, each taking their position as described in the scroll. Ivy could feel the magic in the air intensify, swirling around them as they began to channel their energy into the ritual.

Rowan was the first to speak the incantation, his voice steady and strong. The ancient words resonated through the chamber, lighting up the runes beneath their feet. A soft blue glow spread across the floor, connecting each of them in a web of magical energy.

Aiden followed, his deep voice adding a second layer to the incantation. The glow intensified, growing brighter and more focused. The air around them crackled with power, and Ivy could feel her own magic responding, drawn into the ritual as if the very universe was pulling them together.

Then it was Lysandra's turn. Her voice was soft but sharp, slicing through the heavy air like a blade. The runes around them flared with light, the blue glow deepening into a brilliant sapphire. The magic was building, growing stronger with each word spoken.

Finally, Ivy took a deep breath and began her part of the incantation. Her voice shook at first, but as she continued, she felt the strength of the ritual flow through her. The magic wrapped around them like a protective barrier, shielding them from the darkness that loomed just beyond the temple walls.

The chamber shook violently as the power of the ritual reached its peak. The energy from the Veil surged into the altar, and the room filled with blinding light. For a moment, Ivy thought they had done it—that the ritual had succeeded.

But then, the light dimmed, and a cold, malevolent presence filled the chamber.

From the shadows, a figure emerged—tall, cloaked in darkness, with eyes that burned with the fires of a thousand stars. The Shadow King had arrived.

"So," he said, his voice deep and resonant, echoing through the temple like a thunderstorm. "You think you can stop me with this ancient magic? Pathetic."

Ivy's heart pounded in her chest. The power radiating from the Shadow King was overwhelming, suffocating. But she stood her ground. "We won't let you destroy this world," she said, her voice steady despite the fear that clawed at her insides.

The Shadow King's laughter was cold and cruel. "Destroy it? No, little one. I will reshape it—remake it in my image. And you...you will be the first to fall."

With a wave of his hand, a torrent of dark energy surged toward them. Rowan raised his wand, casting a barrier to shield them, but the force of the attack shattered it instantly, sending them all sprawling to the ground.

Ivy struggled to her feet, the weight of the dark magic pressing down on her like a physical force. But she could not give up now. Not when they were so close.

"The ritual...we have to finish it," she gasped, her voice strained.

Rowan, Aiden, and Lysandra scrambled to their feet, gathering their strength. The magic of the ritual was still there, still waiting for them to complete it. But the Shadow King was too powerful. If they did not find a way to weaken him, they would not stand a chance.

"I have an idea," Lysandra said, her eyes sharp with determination. "We need to bind him—to trap him within the Veil itself."

Aiden looked at her in disbelief. "You are talking about using the Veil as a prison? That is insane! The energy it would take—"

"It's our only option," Lysandra said firmly. "If we don't trap him, he'll destroy us all."

Rowan nodded, understanding. "We will need to alter the ritual. Instead of closing the Veil, we will channel its power into him—bind him to it forever."

Ivy's mind raced. It was a risk—a huge one. But Lysandra was right. If they did not trap the Shadow King, nothing else would matter.

"Let's do it," Ivy said, her voice filled with newfound resolve.

They resumed their positions around the altar, the Scroll of Eternum glowing once more. As they spoke the final incantation, the chamber erupted in light, and the power of the Veil surged through them.

The Shadow King roared in fury, his form beginning to unravel as the magic of the Veil wrapped around him. "You think you can imprison me? You are nothing!"

But the ritual was already in motion. The magic of the Veil bound itself to him, pulling him toward the altar. The darkness that had once filled the chamber was now being drawn into the very heart of the ritual.

With one final scream of rage, the Shadow King was pulled into the Veil, his form disappearing into the swirling energy.

And then, silence.

The light of the ritual faded, and the chamber was still once more. The Veil had held. The Shadow King was gone.

THE ARCANE ACADEMY - THE SHATTERED VEIL

But as Ivy looked at her friends, exhausted but victorious, she knew that this victory had come at a great cost. The Veil was damaged, fragile, and the world would never be the same.

But for now, the final ritual was complete.

The world was safe—at least, for a little while longer.

Chapter 20: The Veil Restored

The world outside the ancient temple seemed frozen in time, as if the land itself was holding its breath. Ivy, Rowan, Aiden, and Lysandra stood amidst the ruins of the altar, their bodies and minds exhausted from the battle against the Shadow King. The air was thick with the scent of magic, both dark and light, and the lingering traces of the final ritual.

For a moment, there was only silence.

"We did it," Rowan said, his voice barely more than a whisper. His wand hung limply in his hand; the toll of the fight evident in the weariness in his eyes. "He's gone."

Ivy wanted to feel the same relief. They had succeeded in defeating the Shadow King and binding him to the Veil, but the strain of the ritual had left the Veil dangerously unstable. She could feel the imbalance in the air, the cracks in the magical fabric that separated their world from the Void.

"Not yet," Lysandra replied, her gaze fixed on the pulsating energy swirling around them. "The Veil is still fractured. We might have bound the Shadow King, but if we do not repair it now, the Void will leak into our world."

Aiden frowned, stepping forward with caution. "I thought the Veil would naturally restore itself. Isn't that how it works?"

"It's too weak," Ivy said softly, sensing the vulnerability in the threads of magic around them. "The Veil is barely holding together. It took too much damage from the Shadow King's attack. If we leave it like this, it will shatter completely."

Rowan ran a hand through his hair, frustration building. "So, what do we do? We barely survived the ritual to bind him. How are we supposed to fix the Veil itself?"

Lysandra stepped toward the altar, determination in her eyes. "The Scroll of Eternum can guide us. There is a second incantation, one designed to restore the Veil after it has been tampered with. But..."

"But it's risky," Ivy finished for her, understanding the unspoken warning.

Lysandra nodded. "It will require more magic than we have ever channeled before. If one of us falters, or if the Veil resists... we could tear it apart completely."

The weight of her words hung heavily in the air. They had just survived a battle against the most powerful dark force in existence, only to be faced with a challenge even more delicate and dangerous. But they had no choice.

Aiden looked at each of them, his usual skepticism replaced by a rare flicker of hope. "We have come this far. We cannot turn back now."

With renewed resolve, they took their places around the altar once more. The Scroll of Eternum hovered above the stone, its ancient runes shimmering faintly. This time, the magic felt different—not as dark or oppressive, but delicate, like threads of silk waiting to be woven together.

Rowan began the chant, his voice steady and sure. The symbols on the scroll glowed brighter, responding to the ancient words of power. The blue light from before returned, spreading across the runes beneath their feet.

Aiden followed, his deep voice filling the chamber as his magic intertwined with Rowan's. The energy in the room intensified, but instead of the harsh, overwhelming force they had felt during the final ritual, this magic was soothing, healing.

Lysandra's voice joined theirs, soft but firm, and the runes around them began to glow a deep violet. The shimmering energy spread from the altar, wrapping itself around the damaged Veil, coaxing it back together, stitch by stitch.

Finally, Ivy closed her eyes and spoke the final incantation. Her words were filled with the magic of the earth, of life itself. She could feel the Veil responding, its edges drawing closer, mending the tears that had threatened to tear the world apart.

The magic swirled around them, filling the chamber with light. Ivy felt a surge of warmth, a sense of peace washing over her as the Veil slowly, but surely, restored itself. The once-fractured barrier between their world and the Void grew stronger, more resilient with each passing second.

And then, with a final flash of brilliant light, the ritual was complete.

The air in the temple grew calm once more, and the glow of the runes faded into nothingness. The Veil was whole again, its fractures sealed, its magic flowing smoothly through the world once more.

Ivy let out a breath she had not realized she had been holding, her body trembling from the effort. "It's done."

Lysandra knelt beside the altar, her hand resting on the cool stone. "The Veil is restored. The Shadow King is bound within it. For now, our world is safe."

Aiden collapsed onto the ground, his chest rising and falling with heavy breaths. "I don't think I've ever been this tired in my life."

Rowan chuckled, though his laugh was tinged with exhaustion. "You're not alone in that."

As the four of them sat together in the quiet aftermath of their victory, Ivy looked out through the temple's broken walls. The sky was beginning to clear, the storm clouds that had loomed over the land for so long finally dissipating. For the first time in what felt like ages, she saw the sun breaking through, its golden rays warming the earth.

A sense of peace settled over her. They had fought harder than they ever thought possible, and they had won. But more than that, they had saved the world from a darkness that could have consumed it entirely.

Still, Ivy knew this was not the end. The Veil had been restored, but the scars left behind by the Shadow King would not fade so easily. There were still secrets to uncover, still mysteries within the Arcane Academy and the Veil itself that needed to be solved.

But for now, they had earned a moment of peace.

As the sun set on the horizon, casting the world in shades of gold and crimson, Ivy turned to her friends, the weight of their shared journey lifting from her shoulders.

Together, they had faced the darkness.

Together, they had restored the Veil.

And together, they would face whatever came next.

Chapter 21: A New Dawn

The sun rose over the horizon, casting a warm glow across the grounds of the Arcane Academy. Ivy stood on the steps of the grand tower, her eyes taking in the serenity of the scene before her. For the first time in months, the academy seemed at peace. The darkness that had once loomed over it was gone, replaced by the gentle hum of life returning to normal.

But nothing would ever be quite the same.

Ivy glanced down at the letter in her hand. It was a summons from the High Council, the governing body that oversaw the balance of magic across the realms. The letter had arrived the previous night, carried by an owl that had swooped down during the celebration.

She had not opened it yet, not because she was afraid of its contents, but because she was not ready to face what came next. After everything they had gone through—the battles, the rituals, the sacrifices—there was a part of her that just wanted to let it all be for a moment longer.

"Big day?" Rowan's voice broke the quiet, and Ivy turned to see him walking toward her, a mischievous grin on his face. His robes were disheveled, as though he had not bothered to change since the previous night's festivities. "I see you've got the Council's attention now."

Ivy managed a small smile. "Seems that way."

"They're probably going to give you some kind of medal," Rowan continued, flopping down beside her on the steps. "Hero of the Veil or something."

Ivy laughed, though the sound was more tired than amused. "Somehow, I don't think that's what they have in mind."

"Well, whatever it is, you deserve it. We all do." He looked out across the academy grounds, the wind ruffling his dark hair. "After everything we went through... it still feels a little unreal, doesn't it?"

Ivy nodded. "It does. But the Veil is restored, the Shadow King is bound, and the academy is safe. That is what matters."

Rowan was quiet for a moment, his expression uncharacteristically serious. "You know this is not the end, right? There is still so much we do not understand about the Veil, about the other realms. We might have won this battle, but the war is not over."

Ivy sighed, her fingers brushing the edges of the letter in her hand. "I know. And that is what worries me."

Before Rowan could respond, Lysandra appeared at the top of the stairs, her silver hair gleaming in the morning sun. She looked more rested than she had in days, but there was a familiar intensity in her violet eyes.

"The Council's waiting for you, Ivy," she said, her voice calm but firm. "They're holding a meeting in the Great Hall."

Ivy stood up, slipping the letter into the pocket of her robes. "I guess it's time to find out what they want."

Rowan got to his feet, brushing the dust off his robes. "We will go with you. Whatever happens next, we are in this together."

Lysandra nodded, stepping forward to join them. "The academy has always been our home, and we have protected it with everything we have. If the Council wants to talk about the future, they will need to hear from all of us."

Ivy felt a swell of gratitude for her friends. Through every trial, every battle, they had stood by her side. Together, they had faced dangers no one else could have survived. And together, they would face whatever came next.

As they made their way to the Great Hall, the corridors of the academy were filled with students and professors, all eager to return to their studies after the long disruption. The air buzzed with excitement, but also a sense of caution. The events of the past few months had left their mark on everyone.

The doors to the Great Hall stood open, and inside, the High Council sat at a long, curved table. Their faces were solemn, and the room was filled with a weighty silence. As Ivy, Rowan, and Lysandra stepped inside, all eyes turned toward them.

Councilor Arlin, a tall man with a commanding presence, was the first to speak. "Ivy Nightshade, Rowan Blackthorn, Lysandra Silverwind—you have done a great service to the academy, and to the entire magical realm. You have restored the Veil, defeated the Shadow King, and protected our world from the Void."

His gaze swept across the room, landing on each of them in turn. "But as you well know, the damage to the Veil has left our world vulnerable. There are still forces at work, dark forces, that seek to exploit the rift between our realms."

Ivy's heart sank. She had known this was coming, but hearing it from the Council made it all too real.

Councilor Arlin continued, his tone grave. "We must ask you to continue your work. The academy needs protectors, and the Veil needs guardians. You are the ones best suited for this task."

Lysandra stepped forward; her chin held high. "We will do whatever it takes to keep the academy safe. But we cannot do it alone."

The Council exchanged glances, and Councilor Arlin nodded. "We understand. That is why we are offering you the title of Keepers of the Veil. You will have access to resources, knowledge, and magic beyond what you have now. But with that title comes great responsibility. You will be tasked with defending the Veil, not just from threats we know, but from those we cannot yet foresee."

Rowan let out a low whistle. "Keepers of the Veil, huh? Sounds intense."

Ivy's mind raced. She had never sought power or titles. All she had ever wanted was to protect the people she cared about. But this—this was something more. A calling. A new path that stretched before her, full of challenges and unknowns.

But she was not afraid.

She looked at Rowan and Lysandra, seeing the same resolve in their eyes. They had already proven they could face the darkness together. Whatever came next, they would face it as one.

Ivy turned back to the Council, her voice steady. "We accept."

The Councilors nodded in approval, and the atmosphere in the room shifted. There was a sense of relief, but also anticipation. The world was changing, and they were stepping into a new era.

As Ivy, Rowan, and Lysandra left the Great Hall, the morning sun shone brightly through the windows, casting long shadows on the marble floors. The academy was alive with the promise of a new day, a new dawn.

Ivy took a deep breath, feeling the warmth of the sun on her face.

This was just the beginning.

Chapter 22: The Legacy of the Veil

As the trio walked out of the Great Hall, the weight of their new roles settled in, but so did the exhilaration. Keepers of the Veil. It was both an honor and a burden, but Ivy, Rowan, and Lysandra were ready. They had faced darkness, betrayal, and impossible odds. Now, the future of the magical realms was in their hands.

Outside, the academy grounds were bustling with life. Students gathered in groups, chattering excitedly about their lessons and the rumors that still swirled around the Veil's restoration. Some whispered about Ivy and her friends, their deeds having become legend in the halls of the Arcane Academy.

"Think this means we'll have to deal with fewer detentions?" Rowan quipped, flashing a grin. "I'm pretty sure Keepers of the Veil get some perks."

Lysandra rolled her eyes, though a smile tugged at her lips. "If anything, we will be held to even higher standards. No more slipping into the restricted sections for you."

"Hey, I was doing research!" Rowan protested, though the glint in his eyes suggested otherwise.

Ivy laughed, feeling a rare moment of lightness in the wake of everything. But the humor could not completely distract her from the growing sense of responsibility. There were still so many unknowns. The Veil had been restored, but the Shadow King's influence lingered, and whispers of other dark forces stirred on the edges of the realms. The Rift had left scars, and those scars might never fully heal.

As they walked, Ivy's thoughts drifted back to their training, their battles, and the friends they had made along the way. Some were no longer with them, fallen in the fight to protect the academy and the realms beyond. Their sacrifices weighed heavily on her, reminding her of the price of magic, of power.

"We need a plan," Lysandra said, her voice cutting through Ivy's reverie. "The Veil is stable for now, but we all felt it—there are forces out there that want to tear it apart. The Shadow King might be gone, but that does not mean we are safe."

"I agree," Ivy replied, her brow furrowed in thought. "The Council gave us resources, but we will need to gather allies. We cannot do this alone."

Rowan nodded. "I have been thinking about that too. There are realms we haven't even touched yet—places were magic works differently. We need to understand them, in case the Veil is breached again."

"Agreed," Lysandra said. "We will need to reach out to the elders in the Elemental Realms, the Seers in the Astral Plains, and maybe even the Draconic Tribes. The more we know, the better we will be prepared."

Ivy considered this for a moment. The world of magic was vast, with realms and forces even the Arcane Academy had barely begun to explore. If they were to protect the Veil, they would need to learn about every threat, every potential ally.

But it was not just knowledge they needed. Ivy thought about her own magic—the way it had evolved during the battle against the Shadow King. She had tapped into something deeper, a power that frightened her as much as it intrigued her. What if that magic was the key to defending the Veil? What if it was the key to unlocking even greater mysteries?

"We'll figure it out," Ivy said softly, more to herself than to her friends. "We always do."

As they continued their walk through the academy grounds, a familiar voice called out from behind them.

"Ivy! Rowan! Lysandra!"

They turned to see Professor Halford striding toward them, his crimson robes billowing in the wind. His expression was serious, but there was a spark of admiration in his eyes.

"I see you've already met with the Council," Halford said, his gaze flicking to the trio. "Keepers of the Veil. Quite the title."

"Yeah, we're still getting used to it," Rowan said, rubbing the back of his neck.

Halford gave a rare smile. "You have earned it. But I wanted to let you know—there is something I have been meaning to show you. Something important."

Ivy raised an eyebrow. "What is it?"

"It's a place, hidden deep within the academy," Halford said, his voice lowering. "Few know of its existence, and fewer still have ever been inside. It is called the Nexus of Eternity. It contains knowledge of the Veil, of the realms beyond, and of magic so ancient that even the High Council has only whispered of it."

Lysandra's eyes widened. "The Nexus of Eternity? I thought that was a myth."

Halford shook his head. "It is very real. And if you are to be the true Keepers of the Veil, you need to see it. There is magic in this world older than any of us can imagine, and if you are to protect the Veil, you must understand its origins."

Ivy felt a chill run down her spine. The Nexus of Eternity. She had heard the name once, in the cryptic notes of an old professor long gone. It was a place of both wonder and danger, a repository of the most powerful and forbidden magics. If it truly existed, it could hold the key to everything they were searching for.

"When do we leave?" Ivy asked, her voice steady.

Halford smiled again, a glint of approval in his eyes. "Now."

As the sun set on the Arcane Academy, Ivy, Rowan, Lysandra, and Professor Halford made their way to the hidden chamber deep beneath the academy. The torches lining the walls flickered with an otherworldly glow, casting long shadows as they descended into the earth.

The air grew colder as they approached an enormous stone door, carved with runes Ivy did not recognize. Halford placed his hand on the door, murmuring an incantation so ancient that the words seemed to vibrate in the air.

The door creaked open, revealing a vast chamber filled with shimmering orbs of light, ancient tomes, and relics from times long forgotten.

"The Nexus of Eternity," Halford said, his voice reverent. "Here, you will find the knowledge of the past, the present, and the future. It is here that your journey as Keepers truly begins."

Ivy stepped forward, her heart pounding in her chest. This was it—their path was clear, but the road ahead was filled with uncertainty. She knew, deep down, that they were on the brink of something far greater than any of them had imagined.

As the doors of the Nexus closed behind them, Ivy realized one thing for certain: their story was far from over. A new dawn had risen, but with it came new challenges, new dangers, and new magic to uncover.

Together, they would face it all. And in doing so, they would shape the future of the magical realms forever.

Chapter 23: The Nexus Unveiled

The chamber within the Nexus of Eternity was unlike anything Ivy had ever seen. Massive, arcane symbols glowed softly on the walls, each one pulsating with ancient energy. The air was thick with magic, a hum that vibrated through her bones and made her skin tingle. There was no mistaking it—this place held power beyond anything she could have imagined.

"Stay close," Professor Halford instructed, leading them deeper into the vast expanse. His voice was calm, but Ivy could sense the weight of what was coming. "The Nexus is alive, in a way. It responds to intent, to purpose. Only those deemed worthy can access its true depths."

Rowan looked around with wide eyes, his usual cocky demeanor replaced by awe. "This place... it feels like the heart of magic itself."

Lysandra nodded; her expression more serious than Ivy had ever seen. "I can feel it too. It is almost like... the Veil is part of this place."

Professor Halford turned to them, his expression grave. "You are not far off, Lysandra. The Nexus was created by the first Keepers of the Veil, eons ago. It is a reservoir of knowledge, but also a safeguard. The magic stored here is connected to the Veil, to the fabric of the realms. If the Veil were to ever collapse entirely, this place would be the last hope of restoring balance."

Ivy swallowed hard. The implications were staggering. "So, if we're going to protect the Veil, we need to understand this place."

"Exactly," Halford said. "But be warned—the Nexus tests those who seek its secrets. It will push you, challenge you, and reveal truths that may be difficult to face."

The words hung in the air, heavy with foreboding. But Ivy knew there was no turning back. They had come too far, fought too hard to protect the Veil, to retreat now.

"Where do we start?" she asked, stepping forward.

Professor Halford gestured toward the center of the chamber, where a large stone altar stood. Upon it rested a single glowing crystal, swirling with every color of the spectrum. "The Heart of the Nexus. Place your hands upon it, and it will reveal to you what you need to see."

Ivy, Rowan, and Lysandra exchanged nervous glances. They had faced the Shadow King, traversed forbidden realms, and unlocked ancient magic—but this felt different. This was a test of their very essence.

Taking a deep breath, Ivy stepped forward first. She reached out, her fingers trembling slightly as they contacted the cool surface of the crystal. Instantly, a surge of magic rushed through her, and the world around her dissolved.

Ivy found herself standing in a place that was both familiar and alien. She was in the Great Hall of the Arcane Academy, but it was shrouded in shadow. The banners hung torn and faded, and the air was thick with an eerie silence.

From the darkness, a figure emerged. It was her—an older version of herself, draped in dark robes, her eyes cold and filled with a power that felt... wrong.

"Is this what you will become?" the older Ivy asked, her voice echoing with menace. "You have the potential to be the greatest Keeper in history—or the one who will doom it all."

Ivy recoiled, her heart racing. "I would never betray the Veil!"

"Would you?" the older Ivy sneered, stepping closer. "Power corrupts, Ivy. The magic you wield, the secrets you uncover—it will change you. Can you trust yourself to resist the darkness?"

Before Ivy could respond, the vision shattered, and she was back in the Nexus, her hand still on the crystal. She pulled away, gasping for breath, her heart pounding in her chest.

"What did you see?" Rowan asked, concern in his voice.

Ivy shook her head, trying to shake off the lingering dread. "I... I am not sure. But whatever it was, it was not good."

Rowan stepped forward next, his face set with determination. As his hand touched the crystal, he too was pulled into the Nexus's magic, his body going rigid as the visions claimed him.

Ivy watched, her mind still reeling from her own encounter. What had the Nexus shown her? Was it a warning, or a glimpse of a possible future? She did not know, but the fear it had instilled in her was real.

After what felt like an eternity, Rowan released the crystal, his eyes wide with shock.

"What did you see?" Ivy asked, her voice barely a whisper.

Rowan's face was pale, his usual bravado nowhere to be found. "I saw... a war. A battle for the Veil, with me leading an army of shadows. It was chaos, Ivy. Pure chaos."

Lysandra's eyes flickered with unease, but she stepped forward without hesitation, placing her hand on the crystal. She stood still for a moment, her brow furrowing in concentration, before quickly pulling back.

"That was... intense," she muttered, rubbing her temples. "I saw the academy in ruins, but I was... alone. Everyone else was gone."

Professor Halford watched them closely, nodding slowly. "The Nexus reveals your greatest fears, your deepest doubts. It is meant to prepare you for the trials ahead. The path of a Keeper is fraught with challenges—many of which will test not just your strength, but your resolve."

Ivy's mind raced. Her vision, Rowan's, and Lysandra's all pointed to a future of turmoil and destruction. But were they warnings of what could be, or simply manifestations of their own fears?

"We need to figure out what this all means," Ivy said, her voice steady despite the unease swirling inside her. "If these visions are trying to tell us something, we need to understand it before it's too late."

Professor Halford nodded. "The Nexus has more to reveal, but its knowledge will not come easily. You have passed the first test, but the real trials are yet to come."

The three of them exchanged grim looks. Whatever lay ahead, it would push them to their limits. But they had come this far, and they were not about to back down now.

With a renewed sense of purpose, Ivy, Rowan, and Lysandra prepared to face the challenges of the Nexus. The fate of the Veil, of the realms, and of the Arcane Academy rested on their shoulders.

And they would not fail.

Chapter 24: The Trials of Unity

The chamber shifted around them once more, the glowing symbols on the walls flickering as the ancient magic prepared for the next trial. Ivy felt the weight of the Nexus pressing down, as if the very air carried the will of the Keepers who had come before them.

Professor Halford stepped back, his face set with the calm patience of someone who had been through this before. "The next trial," he said, "is one of unity. The Nexus tests not only your individual strengths but your ability to work together as one. Only by combining your powers and wills can you unlock the knowledge needed to protect the Veil."

Rowan glanced at Ivy and Lysandra, uncertainty flickering in his eyes. "Great. So now we must trust each other completely, huh?"

Ivy shot him a sidelong look. "You have a problem with that?"

Rowan grinned, though there was an edge to it. "Only when you're bossing me around."

Lysandra rolled her eyes. "We don't have time for this. Whatever is coming, we need to be prepared. Let's just hope it's not as bad as that crystal."

The floor beneath them rumbled, cutting off any further banter. A circular pattern emerged from the center of the chamber, glowing with ethereal light. As it expanded, an enormous stone doorway materialized before them, its surface etched with intricate carvings. Strange runes twisted and pulsed, and beyond the door, a thick veil of mist obscured what lay ahead.

THE ARCANE ACADEMY - THE SHATTERED VEIL

"This is it," Professor Halford said softly. "The Nexus will now test your bond—your ability to function as one. If you fail, the door will not open, and the knowledge within will remain forever sealed."

Rowan exhaled sharply. "No pressure then."

Without another word, Ivy, Rowan, and Lysandra stepped toward the door. The closer they came, the more intense the magic around them grew, thickening the air with a tangible force. Ivy could feel it tugging at her, searching for any weaknesses in their connection.

As they stood before the door, the runes began to glow brighter, and a voice echoed through the chamber, deep and resonant, as though coming from the heart of the Nexus itself.

"Three paths converge—three hearts entwined in fate. Together, you must act as one, or be consumed by the darkness that seeks to divide."

The mist beyond the door swirled, revealing three separate paths, each one shrouded in mystery. Ivy felt a chill run down her spine. They had to choose, and yet, it seemed impossible.

"What do we do?" Lysandra asked, her eyes scanning the twisting routes.

"I don't think it's about choosing one path," Ivy said slowly. "I think we're supposed to take all three."

Rowan blinked. "Wait, split up? I thought we were supposed to stay together."

Ivy shook her head. "No, not split up. I think we need to move forward as individuals, but remain connected somehow. Like Professor Halford said—unity. We have to act as one, even if we're apart."

Professor Halford's voice came from behind them, steady and reassuring. "Ivy's right. You must trust in each other, even when you cannot see or hear one another. Your bond must transcend distance."

Rowan hesitated; his brow furrowed. "So, we just... walk down these paths and hope for the best?"

Lysandra placed a hand on his shoulder. "We'll figure it out. We always do."

With that, Ivy stepped toward the first path. As her foot crossed the threshold, she felt a wave of energy pass over her, and the mist closed in, separating her from the others.

For a moment, Ivy panicked. The mist was thick, and she could not see more than a few feet in front of her. But she forced herself to stay calm. This was part of the trial. She had to trust that Rowan and Lysandra were still with her, even if she could not see them.

The path before her wound through the dense fog, and strange shapes flitted at the edge of her vision. Shadows, dark and ominous, moved just out of reach, whispering in an unfamiliar language. Ivy's heart raced, but she pushed forward, focusing on her connection to the others.

"I trust them," she whispered to herself. "We've been through worse than this."

As if in response to her words, the shadows receded, and the path straightened. Ivy felt a surge of hope. She could do this. They could do this.

Meanwhile, Rowan's path was vastly different. The moment he stepped into the mist, he found himself surrounded by fire. The heat was intense, and flames licked at his heels as he ran, trying to avoid the searing tongues of magic.

"Great," he muttered, dodging another burst of flame. "This is just what I needed."

Despite the danger, Rowan could feel a strange connection pulling at him, guiding his steps. He knew it was not just his own instincts—it was something deeper. Ivy's determination, Lysandra's calm resolve... it was as if their emotions were blending with his own, helping him push forward.

"Alright, I get it," he grumbled to no one in particular. "Unity or burn alive. Got it."

Lysandra's path was the most serene, yet unsettling. She walked through a forest of crystal trees, their branches humming with an eerie melody. The air was cold, and the ground beneath her shimmered with frost. But despite the beauty, there was a deep sense of unease. The trees seemed to watch her, their crystalline eyes glowing with unnatural light.

She reached out with her magic, trying to sense Ivy and Rowan. It was faint, but she could feel them—like distant stars in a vast sky. It was enough to keep her grounded, to remind her that they were all connected, even in this strange place.

"We're almost there," she whispered. "Just hold on."

Finally, after what felt like hours, the three paths converged once more. The mist parted, revealing a circular platform at the heart of the Nexus. Ivy, Rowan, and Lysandra stood together again, the sense of unity between them stronger than ever.

The stone doorway before them shimmered, the runes glowing brightly. The voice of the Nexus returned; its tone reverent.

"You have passed the Trial of Unity. The bond between you is strong, forged in the fires of trust and tempered by the strength of your hearts."

The doorway creaked open, revealing a vast library of knowledge beyond. Scrolls, books, and ancient artifacts lined the walls, each one filled with the secrets of the Keepers and the power of the Veil.

Ivy felt a sense of awe wash over her. This was what they had been searching for—the knowledge they needed to protect the Veil and face whatever darkness was coming.

But as they stepped forward, Ivy could not shake the feeling that this was only the beginning. The true test was still ahead.

Chapter 25: The Trial of Flames

As Ivy, Rowan, and Lysandra stepped into the ancient library, they could feel the palpable weight of the knowledge that surrounded them. The air buzzed with old, forgotten magic, and every book and scroll seemed to whisper, beckoning them deeper into the labyrinth of lore. However, the moment they entered, the door behind them slammed shut with a deafening thud.

"This can't be good," Rowan muttered, glancing at the now sealed entrance.

The library stretched endlessly ahead of them, twisting into shadowed alcoves and towering shelves of arcane tomes. Faint, flickering lights floated in the air, casting eerie glows on the rows of ancient texts. A large, central staircase spiraled downwards into darkness, while above, crystal chandeliers seemed to pulse with magic.

Ivy turned toward the others; her voice steady but cautious. "I have a feeling that we're not just here to read. There's more magic at work in this place."

Suddenly, the lights dimmed, and the room shook with a low, guttural growl. The walls began to shift, the bookshelves rearranging themselves into a spiraling labyrinth. Runes flared to life on the floor, glowing with a fiery orange hue. The air became hot, and Ivy could feel the tingle of magic crawling across her skin.

Before them, a massive stone door materialized out of thin air, engraved with a blazing symbol of a phoenix rising from flames. Above the door, ancient words etched themselves into the stone: **"The Trial of Flames: Only Those Who Can Harness the Fire May Proceed."**

Rowan groaned. "Flames? Again? Why is it always fire?"

Lysandra's eyes narrowed. "This isn't just fire, Rowan. It is phoenix fire—one of the most powerful forms of elemental magic. We need to be careful."

Ivy approached the door cautiously, her hand hovering just above the runes. "We've come this far. Whatever the trial is, we face it together."

Without hesitation, the door swung open, revealing a vast chamber of molten lava and floating platforms of stone. The heat was unbearable, even at the entrance. At the far end of the chamber, a towering statue of a phoenix loomed, its eyes burning with intense flame. Above the statue, a glowing orb of fire levitated, pulsing with energy.

"The Flame of the Phoenix," Ivy whispered. "It's a test of endurance and magic."

Rowan glanced at the platforms of stone that floated precariously over the bubbling lava. "Great. So, we just must avoid getting burned alive and make it to the other side. No problem."

Lysandra stepped forward, her eyes scanning the room. "This is no ordinary trial. The platforms will shift, and the flames will rise. We'll need to use our magic to navigate through."

Just as she spoke, the first platform began to move, shifting slowly away from the entrance. Without hesitation, Ivy summoned a gust of wind, propelling herself onto the platform with graceful ease.

"Follow my lead!" Ivy called out.

Rowan and Lysandra leaped after her, their magic flaring to life as they soared across the platforms. But no sooner had they landed on the first platform than the room reacted violently. Jets of fire shot up from the lava below, and the platforms began to move faster, zigzagging unpredictably through the chamber.

"Stay focused!" Lysandra shouted as she conjured a shield of ice to block an oncoming wave of flame. The heat was so intense that the ice sizzled, but it held firm long enough for them to move forward.

Rowan, ever the quick thinker, raised his hand and channeled his own magic, creating a barrier of shadow that absorbed the brunt of the flames. "I'm getting really tired of fire," he muttered, wiping the sweat from his brow.

As they made their way across the treacherous platforms, the challenges grew more intense. Lava geysers erupted randomly, and fiery creatures made of molten rock began to emerge from the depths below, leaping onto the platforms to block their path.

Ivy drew her wand and sent a pulse of wind magic crashing into one of the creatures, shattering it into pieces. "They're drawn to the magic! We need to keep moving!"

Lysandra summoned a spear of water, hurling it at another creature that leapt toward her, turning it into steam with a hiss. "Keep your spells ready!"

But the closer they got to the phoenix statue, the more chaotic the room became. The platforms began to tilt dangerously, and the lava surged higher, licking at the edges of their stone footing. The fiery orb above the phoenix statue began to glow even brighter, casting an oppressive heat throughout the chamber.

Rowan wiped the sweat from his brow, his breath coming in heavy gasps. "We're not going to make it at this pace. There is too much heat, and the platforms are moving too fast!"

Ivy's mind raced. There had to be a way to control the fire, to use the magic in the room to their advantage. Then, it hit her.

"Phoenix fire is alive!" Ivy shouted. "It reacts to strength and willpower. We need to control it, not fight it!"

Rowan raised an eyebrow. "And how do we control fire that's trying to incinerate us?"

Ivy reached deep within herself, drawing on the power of the wind she had mastered. But instead of using it to fight the flames, she began to shape it, gently coaxing the fire around them to bend to her will. Slowly, the flames began to respond, parting just enough for them to continue forward.

Lysandra caught on quickly, raising her own magic. Instead of creating ice to block the flames, she transformed the water into steam, guiding the heat away from their path.

Rowan, ever the trickster, used his shadow magic to redirect the fire's intensity, creating pockets of cooler air as they dashed across the final platforms.

As they reached the base of the phoenix statue, the fiery creatures swarmed around them, but Ivy's newfound control over the flames held them at bay. She turned her attention to the glowing orb above the statue, her heart racing.

"We need to harness the Flame of the Phoenix," Ivy said, her voice resolute. "It's the key to completing the trial."

With a deep breath, Ivy raised her hands toward the orb, channeling every ounce of her magic. The wind around her swirled, mixing with the flames as she summoned the power of the phoenix itself. The orb pulsed, and for a moment, Ivy could feel the raw, ancient power of the fire surging through her.

Rowan and Lysandra stood beside her, adding their own magic to the mix. Together, they poured their energy into the orb, their connection stronger than ever. The room shook violently as the power of the phoenix responded to their call.

Suddenly, the orb exploded with light, filling the chamber with a brilliant glow. The flames that had once threatened to consume them receded, and the fiery creatures vanished into the molten lava below.

The trial was over.

As the light faded, the stone platforms settled, and the oppressive heat lifted. The door on the other side of the chamber creaked open, revealing the path forward.

Rowan let out a long breath. "Well, that was fun. What is next? A blizzard?"

Ivy smiled, her heart still racing from the intensity of the trial. "Whatever it is, we're ready."

Lysandra nodded; her eyes gleaming with determination. "Let's see what the Nexus has in store for us next."

And with that, they stepped through the doorway, ready for whatever challenge awaited them.

Chapter 26: The Crystal Cavern

As the trio stepped through the doorway, the heat from the Trial of Flames gave way to a sudden chill. A cold draft blew past them, carrying the scent of damp earth and something ancient. Before them, a dimly lit tunnel stretched into the depths of the mountain, its walls glittering faintly with minerals embedded in the stone.

Ivy rubbed her arms, feeling the sharp contrast in temperature. "This place feels... different."

Rowan stepped cautiously beside her, his hand resting on the hilt of his wand. "Yeah, it's got that creepy, ancient vibe. Like we've just walked into the belly of some slumbering beast."

Lysandra, her eyes scanning the passage ahead, seemed unphased by the chill. "I've read about these places in the archives. It is a crystal cavern, were raw magical energy flows freely. The crystals here are conduits for power, amplifying spells—if you can control them."

Ivy's gaze followed Lysandra's words. "And if we can't?"

"Then the magic here could overwhelm us," Lysandra replied, her voice edged with caution.

The deeper they ventured into the cavern, the brighter the crystals became, shimmering with every step. But it was not long before the natural beauty of the cavern shifted into something more foreboding. Strange echoes bounced off the walls—whispers of things unseen, and the ground beneath their feet began to tremble slightly.

"That's never a good sign," Rowan muttered as the trembling grew stronger.

Suddenly, the cavern opened into a massive underground chamber. Stalactites hung from the ceiling, dripping water into a vast lake of shimmering, glowing liquid. Across the lake, they could see an island, and at its center stood an enormous crystal formation, radiating magical energy so intense that the air around it seemed to hum.

"That crystal," Ivy whispered, her eyes wide with awe. "It's like nothing I've ever seen before."

Lysandra nodded, her expression a mix of excitement and concern. "It's a power crystal—pure, untainted energy. If we can harness it, it could give us the strength we need to face whatever is coming. But if we mishandle it, it could tear us apart."

Rowan scratched his head. "Right. So, how do we get across that glowing death-lake without turning into magical dust?"

As if in response, the lake began to ripple. The glowing liquid swirled, and a soft rumble echoed through the chamber. The water began to rise, forming into shapes—humanoid figures made entirely of the glowing liquid.

Lysandra stepped back, her eyes narrowing. "We have to be careful. Those are not just magical creatures—they are manifestations of the crystal's energy. If they touch us, they'll drain our magic and leave us defenseless."

Rowan raised his wand, already summoning a protective shield. "Okay, that's terrifying."

Ivy, thinking quickly, stepped forward and focused her energy. "If these creatures are made of magic, we can manipulate the flow of energy around them."

Concentrating on the nearest creature, Ivy summoned a gust of wind, trying to disrupt its form. To her relief, the creature wavered, its body swirling and breaking apart before dissolving back into the lake.

"It worked!" Ivy called out, but her moment of triumph was short-lived. Dozens more of the glowing figures rose from the lake, surrounding them on all sides.

Lysandra's eyes darted between the creatures and the island in the center of the lake. "We don't have time to fight all of them. We need to get to that crystal."

Ivy glanced at the creatures, then back at the glowing lake. "We need a way across..."

Rowan grinned suddenly, a mischievous glint in his eyes. "I have an idea. Hold on tight!"

Before Ivy could ask what, he meant, Rowan thrust his wand toward the ground, muttering a series of quick, sharp words under his breath. A wave of shadow magic surged outward, enveloping the three of them. The world around them went dark for a moment, and when the darkness faded, they found themselves standing on the island at the center of the lake.

Ivy blinked in shock. "Rowan, that was—"

"Brilliant? I know," Rowan said with a wink, though the strain of the spell was evident in his voice.

The crystal loomed before them now, its size more intimidating up close. It pulsed with magic, almost like it had a heartbeat, and the energy radiating from it was overwhelming.

"We need to synchronize our magic," Lysandra said. "The crystal will amplify whatever we channel into it, but if we're not careful, it could destabilize and... well, let's just say we wouldn't survive."

Ivy nodded, stepping forward. "Let's do this."

The three of them raised their wands in unison, focusing their magic toward the crystal. Ivy called on the wind, summoning a powerful vortex of air that wrapped around the crystal. Lysandra conjured a stream of water, weaving it through the air like a flowing ribbon of energy, and Rowan added his shadow magic, creating a protective barrier around the vortex.

As their combined magic connected with the crystal, it flared to life, glowing brighter and brighter until the entire cavern was filled with blinding light. The ground shook violently, and the air crackled with raw power. For a moment, it felt as if the magic might tear them apart, but then, just as quickly as it had begun, the light faded.

The crystal's glow dimmed, and the intense magic in the air subsided.

Ivy lowered her wand, her heart still racing. "Did we... did we succeed?"

Lysandra inspected the crystal, her eyes widening. "Not only did we stabilize it, but we've absorbed its power. The magic is now a part of us."

Rowan, still catching his breath, gave a weary smile. "So, what does that mean? Are we supercharged wizards now?"

Lysandra shook her head, her expression serious. "It means we're stronger—but it also means the challenges ahead will be even more dangerous."

As if on cue, the cavern rumbled again, and the crystal began to shift. The platform they stood on trembled, and the lake below started to bubble furiously.

Ivy's eyes widened. "We need to get out of here—now!"

With no time to waste, they dashed toward the edge of the island, where the glowing lake began to rise, the energy manifesting into larger, more menacing creatures. But with the power of the crystal now flowing through them, Ivy, Rowan, and Lysandra were ready for what lay ahead.

The true challenge had only just begun.

Chapter 27: The Awakening of the Ancients

The trio barely escaped the crumbling crystal cavern as they sprinted toward the exit, magical creatures rising behind them, chasing their every step. The rush of energy from the newly absorbed magic flowed through their veins, making each movement faster, sharper, and more in tune with their surroundings. But it was not just a new sense of power—it was a responsibility that weighed on them heavily.

Ivy's heart pounded as they emerged from the cave, the eerie glow of the magic-lit sky framing the horizon in unnatural colors. The entire landscape felt more alive, more intense, as if the world itself had awoken from a deep slumber. They paused just outside the entrance, catching their breath. Ivy glanced back, still feeling the hum of the cavern's raw energy.

"That... was insane," Rowan panted, leaning on his knees. "And we're not dead. I'm going to count that as a win."

Lysandra's eyes were fixed on the horizon. Her usually calm demeanor was gone, replaced by a look of unease. "We've tapped into something ancient. Something far more powerful than we understand."

Ivy nodded. "I felt it too. It's like we've woken something up... something that's been waiting."

Rowan frowned. "You mean the crystal? Or...?"

Lysandra shook her head slowly. "Not just the crystal. The entire realm. The magic we absorbed—it is connected to something much bigger. And now it's stirred."

A sudden tremor shook the ground beneath their feet, cutting off any further discussion. It was not like the shifting of the earth they had experienced in the cavern. This was different—an unsettling vibration that seemed to resonate deep in the earth. In the distance, the sky darkened further, swirling with unnatural clouds that blotted out what little light remained.

"Something's coming," Ivy whispered.

The earth trembled again, more violently this time. Then, as if to confirm Ivy's fear, an enormous roar echoed across the sky. It was a deep, resonating sound that seemed to come from the core of the world itself, shaking the mountains and sending birds scattering in the distance.

Lysandra's face paled. "The Ancients. They've awakened."

Rowan's eyes widened in disbelief. "The Ancients? You mean the old myths? The guardians of the world's primal magic? I thought they were just legends!"

"They were," Lysandra said, her voice low. "Until now."

Suddenly, the ground split open in front of them. From the gaping chasm, towering stone creatures emerged—golems, their bodies carved from the earth itself, their eyes glowing with ancient power. Each step they took reverberated through the ground, shaking the trees and cracking the soil beneath their massive feet.

"We need to move!" Ivy shouted, raising her wand instinctively.

But the golems were not their only problem. From the sky, dark-winged figures began to descend, their black feathers glistening in the dim light. They were the Shadow singers, ancient creatures known to follow the will of the Ancients, their voices said to drive any who listened into madness.

Rowan's grip tightened on his wand. "Great. Flying death crows. This day just keeps getting better."

Lysandra looked between the golems and the Shadow singers. "We can't fight them all. Not here, not like this."

"We don't have a choice!" Ivy said, preparing to defend themselves.

But Lysandra was already forming a plan. "No, listen. We need to head to the temple. The Temple of the First Magic. It is where the Ancients' magic was first sealed. If we can reach it, we might be able to stop whatever's coming."

Ivy hesitated, watching as the stone golems drew closer, their footsteps shaking the very ground they stood on. "Are you sure? What if we cannot stop them?"

Lysandra's eyes were determined. "It's the only chance we have."

Rowan raised his wand, creating a swirling vortex of shadow magic to shield them from the golems' approach. "Then we run. Now."

Without another word, they dashed toward the nearest path, away from the stone monstrosities. The ground continued to tremble, and the roars of the Ancients echoed in the distance, each one more terrifying than the last. The Shadow singers swooped overhead, but Rowan's shadow shield kept them at bay for the moment.

As they ran, Ivy felt the weight of the magic they carried pressing harder on her soul. It was growing more intense, the power within her building to a dangerous level. She glanced at Lysandra, who seemed equally strained. Rowan, too, was fighting to maintain control of his powers, his shadow magic flickering like a flame about to burn out of control.

"The temple's not far," Lysandra said through gritted teeth, "but we need to be prepared. The Ancients won't let us approach without a fight."

Ivy nodded, though she could feel the fatigue settling in. "Whatever it takes. We can't let this world fall."

The trio pressed forward, the weight of their newfound magic pulling at them with every step. Behind them, the stone golems and Shadow singers pursued relentlessly, but the temple lay just beyond the horizon—a faint glimmer of hope in an otherwise darkening world.

As they neared their destination, they could sense the ancient magic pulsing through the earth, calling to the power they had absorbed. It was time to face the greatest challenge yet.

The Ancients had awoken—and only Ivy, Rowan, and Lysandra stood in the way of their wrath.

Chapter 28: The Temple of the First Magic

The trio finally reached the edge of the forest, emerging into a wide, barren clearing. In the center stood the Temple of the First Magic—a towering, ancient structure made of black stone, covered in intricate carvings that pulsed with faint light. The air around it buzzed with power, and the ground itself seemed to hum with energy. Vines twisted around its pillars, their roots glowing with magical essence as if the temple had been alive for centuries, just waiting for someone to awaken its ancient force.

Ivy, Rowan, and Lysandra stopped to catch their breath. The path to the temple was open, but the feeling in the air was thick with tension, and they knew this would be their last stand.

Rowan wiped the sweat from his brow. "Is it just me, or does this place scream 'bad idea'?"

Ivy shook her head, her heart racing with a mix of fear and determination. "It's our only chance. If we don't get inside, the Ancients will tear the world apart."

Lysandra's gaze was fixed on the temple, her voice barely a whisper. "The magic here... it's unlike anything I've ever felt. It is raw, pure. But it's dangerous."

The ground trembled again, but this time, it was not the Ancients approaching—it was the pulse of the magic inside the temple, reacting to their presence.

"We don't have much time," Lysandra said, motioning toward the entrance. "Once we step inside, the magic will test us. Only those worthies can wield the First Magic. If we fail, we'll be consumed."

Rowan smirked, though there was little humor in his eyes. "Oh great, just what we need. Another test."

Ivy stepped forward, leading the group toward the temple's entrance. As they crossed the threshold, the atmosphere changed immediately. The air inside was thick, almost oppressive, and every footstep echoed through the vast hall. The interior was vast, with towering pillars and a ceiling that seemed to stretch into infinity. Ancient symbols glowed faintly on the walls, shifting, and changing as they passed.

At the far end of the hall stood an altar, and above it floated a massive orb of swirling energy—the heart of the First Magic. Its power radiated throughout the room, a chaotic storm of light and shadow.

"The Heart of the First Magic," Lysandra whispered. "It's alive."

Suddenly, a deep voice echoed through the hall, reverberating through the stone walls. "Who dares to enter the Temple of the First Magic?"

The trio froze as an ethereal figure appeared before them, cloaked in robes of shadow and light. Its eyes gleamed with ancient knowledge, and its presence filled the room with a sense of both awe and dread.

"We seek to restore balance," Ivy said, stepping forward despite the weight of the figure's presence. "The Ancients have awoken, and the world is in danger."

The figure's gaze bore into them, unblinking. "The magic you carry is both your strength and your curse. It binds you to this realm, but it also threatens to destroy you. To wield the First Magic, you must prove yourselves worthy."

Rowan glanced at Ivy and Lysandra. "Here we go again."

The figure raised its hand, and the temple shifted around them. The walls dissolved into swirling mist, and suddenly, they were no longer standing in the hall. Instead, they found themselves in a vast, endless void, with nothing but the Heart of the First Magic hovering before them.

The voice echoed again. "Face the trial of the First Magic. Prove that your will is stronger than the power that seeks to consume you."

Ivy felt the weight of the magic pulling at her, trying to overwhelm her senses. The power was intoxicating, filling her mind with visions of endless possibilities, but she knew that giving in would mean losing herself.

Rowan gripped his wand, his shadow magic flaring around him in a protective shield. "This... this is insane."

Lysandra's eyes were closed, her hands glowing with a soft light as she focused on keeping her mind clear. "We can do this. We just need to stay grounded. Don't let the magic take over."

The Heart of the First Magic pulsed with energy, sending waves of power crashing toward them. Ivy felt her knees buckle as the force of the magic hit her, but she gritted her teeth and pushed back with her own willpower.

"We have to stay together," she shouted over the roar of the magic. "Don't let it break us!"

Rowan struggled to keep his shadow shield intact, but the power of the First Magic was relentless, tearing at his defenses. "Easier said than done!"

Lysandra's light magic flared brightly as she fought against the pull of the magic, her face strained with effort. "Focus! We are stronger than this!"

The void around them twisted and warped, and Ivy realized that the trial was not just about their magic—it was testing their very essence, their will to resist the temptation of ultimate power.

As the magic swirled around them, Ivy reached deep within herself, drawing on the strength she had gained through all their trials. She was not just fighting for herself—she was fighting for her friends, for the world, for everything they had worked to protect.

With a final surge of determination, she pushed back against the magic, forcing it to bend to her will. The void trembled, and the Heart of the First Magic flickered.

Rowan and Lysandra followed her lead, channeling their own power to resist the pull of the magic. Together, their combined strength formed a barrier of light and shadow, pushing the chaotic energy back toward the Heart.

The voice echoed once more, but this time, there was a note of approval in its tone. "You have proven your worth."

The void dissolved, and the trio found themselves back in the temple hall. The Heart of the First Magic still floated above the altar, but now its glow was softer, more controlled.

"You are the chosen ones," the voice said. "The First Magic is now yours to command. Use it wisely, for the fate of the world rests in your hands."

Ivy, Rowan, and Lysandra exchanged a glance, their faces filled with awe and relief. They had passed the trial. But the battle was far from over.

The Ancients were still out there, and the final confrontation was drawing near.

As they stepped forward to claim the power of the First Magic, they knew that the true test was yet to come.

Chapter 29: The Ancients' Awakening

The wind howled through the forest as Ivy, Rowan, and Lysandra stepped out of the Temple of the First Magic. Their victory in the trial felt like a dream, but the weight of the power they now carried was undeniable. It pulsed within them, each of their steps resonating with the energy of the ancient force now under their command.

But there was no time to revel in their success. Dark clouds churned in the sky above, unnatural, and ominous. The air itself felt charged with tension, and the ground trembled as if the world was bracing for something terrible.

Rowan glanced at the sky, his eyes narrowing. "We're too late. They're waking up."

Lysandra's face paled as she focused on the horizon. "The Ancients. They're coming."

Ivy gripped her staff tighter, feeling the magic surge through her veins, but it brought her little comfort. The Ancients, beings of immense power from a time long forgotten, were rising again. Their fury, locked away for eons, was now unleashed upon the world.

"We need to move fast," Ivy said, her voice steady despite the growing fear inside her. "We have the First Magic, but we're not ready for them. Not yet."

Suddenly, the ground beneath them shook violently, knocking them off balance. From the earth, enormous stone figures began to emerge—monstrous shapes that towered over the forest, their forms carved from the very land itself. Their eyes burned with a deep, ancient fire, and their movements were slow but deliberate, as if waking from a long slumber.

"Go!" Ivy shouted as the ground erupted around them, fissures splitting the earth. "We can't fight them here!"

They broke into a run, weaving through the trees as the stone giants lumbered after them. The forest itself seemed to come alive with the awakening of the Ancients. Trees twisted and cracked, their roots pulling free from the ground as the earth itself groaned in protest.

"We have to get to the city!" Lysandra called out, her breath coming in gasps as she struggled to keep up. "It's the only place with defenses strong enough to hold them back!"

Rowan's face was set in grim determination. "The city won't stand for long, not against this."

But there was no other choice. The heart of Arcane Academy, and the capital city surrounding it, was the last bastion of hope. Its magical defenses were the most powerful in the realm, and if the Ancients were to destroy it, there would be nothing left to stop them.

As they ran, Ivy could feel the power of the First Magic thrumming inside her, begging to be used. But she knew they could not risk it yet. Not until they understood its true potential. One wrong move, and the magic could consume them just as easily as it had empowered them.

They burst out of the forest; the sprawling city visible in the distance. Its towering spires and glowing wards stood as a beacon of hope in the darkening sky. But already, she could see the chaos within the city's walls. Smoke rose from various points, and flashes of magic illuminated the distant streets.

"They've already reached the city," Ivy said, her heart sinking.

Rowan shook his head, his jaw clenched. "We're running out of time."

Without hesitation, they pressed on, their minds racing with the weight of what was to come. The Ancients were more powerful than anything they had ever faced, and now, the fate of the entire world rested on their shoulders.

But the power of the First Magic had chosen them for a reason. And as they approached the city gates, Ivy made a silent vow. She would not let the Ancients destroy everything they held dear.

"Prepare yourselves," she said as they neared the city's defenses, the sounds of battle already filling the air. "The real fight starts now."

With a final glance at her companions, Ivy led the charge into the fray, the magic of the First Magic crackling around them like a storm ready to break. The Ancients were rising, but so too were the last defenders of the world. And in the coming battle, only one side would prevail.

Chapter 30: The Last Stand

The city of Arcane Academy was in chaos. Towers crumbled, the magical wards flickered and faltered, and the air was thick with smoke and the echoes of battle. The Ancients, colossal and indomitable, had breached the outer defenses and were advancing relentlessly toward the heart of the city.

Ivy, Rowan, and Lysandra stood at the edge of the Grand Plaza, where the Academy's most powerful magical barrier still held, though it wavered under the relentless assault. Beyond the barrier, towering figures of stone and shadow tore through the city streets, their eyes glowing with ancient fury. Behind them, a storm of dark clouds churned, crackling with energy, as if the heavens themselves were reacting to the upheaval.

"We're running out of time," Lysandra said, her voice trembling but resolute.

Rowan gripped his staff tightly. "No more running. This is it."

Ivy nodded, her heart racing but her resolve stronger than ever. "We fight here. We stop them."

The Heart of the First Magic pulsed within them, filling them with immense power. But with that power came a dangerous temptation—the urge to unleash it all, to obliterate the Ancients in one final strike. Yet, Ivy knew that doing so could destroy everything, including themselves.

"We can't afford to lose control," Ivy warned, looking at her friends. "We need to be smart about this. The Ancients are too powerful to defeat by brute force."

Rowan's expression softened; his typical bravado replaced by a rare moment of sincerity. "We've made it this far. We can do this—together."

Ivy raised her staff, the air around it crackling with energy as she channeled the First Magic. "Together."

The ground trembled beneath their feet as the largest of the Ancients—a towering, monstrous figure with burning eyes and a crown of jagged stone—approached the plaza. Its voice rumbled like thunder, shaking the very foundations of the city.

"Mortals, your time has come. Surrender to the will of the Ancients, or be destroyed."

Ivy stepped forward; her voice steady but filled with the authority of the First Magic. "We will never surrender. This world doesn't belong to you anymore."

The Ancient roared, raising its massive arm to strike, but Ivy was already in motion. She unleashed a wave of magical energy, not to destroy, but to bind. The magic wrapped around the Ancient's arm, slowing its movement.

"Rowan, now!" Ivy shouted.

Rowan did not hesitate. He called upon the shadows, his magic entwining with Ivy's, and together, they forced the ancient back. The creature's roar shook the plaza, but it could not break free.

Lysandra joined them, her light magic flaring as she cast a barrier of protection around them. "We can't hold it forever!" she warned, her voice strained.

The Ancient's resistance grew, and cracks began to form in the ground beneath their feet. The other Ancients, sensing their leader's struggle, turned their attention to the trio, their movements slow but terrifying.

"Ivy!" Rowan yelled, struggling to maintain his hold. "What's the plan?"

Ivy's mind raced. They had the power of the First Magic, but raw power alone was not enough. The Ancients were too deeply tied to the world, their very existence a part of the natural order. Destroying them completely would upset the balance of magic itself.

Then it hit her—the realization that had eluded them until now.

"We're not supposed to destroy them!" Ivy exclaimed, her eyes widening. "We need to bind them back to the earth!"

Lysandra's face lit up in understanding. "Of course! The Ancients are part of the world's magic. They were never meant to be erased—just sealed."

"But how?" Rowan asked, still wrestling with the Ancient's force.

Ivy drew on the knowledge the First Magic had given her. The Ancients had been bound before, ages ago, by the magic of the world itself. They could do the same—but only if they worked together, in perfect harmony with the First Magic.

"We'll use the First Magic to create a new seal," Ivy said, her voice filled with determination. "But we need to focus all of our energy on binding them, not fighting them."

The trio quickly formed a circle, their magic intertwining as they poured their will into the earth beneath them. The ground responded, glowing with ancient runes as the power of the First Magic spread out from their circle, weaving through the city like roots of light and shadow.

The Ancients roared in defiance, but the magic was too strong. Slowly, the towering figures were drawn back toward the ground, their immense forms turning to stone as the binding spell took hold.

The largest Ancient, the leader, struggled the most. It fought against the magic, its eyes burning with rage. But Ivy, Rowan, and Lysandra held firm, their combined strength pushing it back.

With a final, deafening roar, the leader of the Ancients collapsed, its form turning to stone as it was bound once more to the earth. The dark clouds overhead began to dissipate, and the tremors in the ground ceased.

The city was silent.

Ivy lowered her staff, her body trembling with exhaustion. The weight of what they had done—what they had survived—settled over her like a heavy cloak.

"It's over," Rowan said quietly, his voice filled with disbelief.

Lysandra wiped a tear from her cheek, a smile breaking through the exhaustion. "We did it."

The Heart of the First Magic still pulsed within them, but its energy was calm now, at peace. The world was safe, and the balance had been restored.

As the trio stood in the Grand Plaza, surrounded by the remnants of the battle, Ivy knew that this was not the end of their journey. The magic they carried would continue to be a part of them, and the world would always need protectors.

But for now, they had earned their rest.

"We'll rebuild," Ivy said, looking out over the city. "The Academy, the world... everything. We'll make it stronger."

Rowan grinned, though he was barely able to stand. "And maybe take a long vacation."

Lysandra laughed, the sound a relief after the tension of the battle. "I think we've earned that."

Together, they walked toward the heart of the city, knowing that whatever challenges lay ahead, they would face them together. The Ancients were bound once more, and the world had a chance to heal.

The Arcane Academy had survived, and with it, a new dawn of magic had begun.

Don't miss out!

Visit the website below and you can sign up to receive emails whenever Kirsten Yates publishes a new book. There's no charge and no obligation.

https://books2read.com/r/B-A-WIEEC-TJDJF

BOOKS 2 READ

Connecting independent readers to independent writers.

Also by Kirsten Yates

Forget Me Not
Forget Me Not
Forget Me Not

The Arcane Academy
The Arcane Academy
The Arcane Academy - The Chronicle Of The Lost Arcane
The Arcane Academy - The Weavers Gamit
The Arcane Academy - The Shattered Veil

Standalone
Last summer love
Lily and the bubblegum balloon
The Storm Of Shadows